TIDES

A STORY COLLECTION

Liminal Books

Liminal Books is an imprint of Between the Lines Publishing. The Liminal Books name and logo are trademarks of Between the Lines Publishing.

Cover Photo by Morgan Bliadd

Between the Lines Publishing
1769 Lexington Ave N, Ste 286
Roseville MN 55113
btwnthelines.com

First Published: September 2024

ISBN: (Paperback) 978-1-965059-08-1

ISBN: (Ebook) 978-1-965059-09-8

TIDES

Bill Mesce, Jr.

Table of Contents

140 OVER 90

Lloyd didn't know how long Miriam had been standing in the living room archway but when he heard her long, slightly disgusted sigh, he had the impression it had been a while.

"You're overdue," she said.

"Again, with this?"

"I got a second email from the doctors. And a text. And a phone call. You're overdue."

"I'm fine."

"Go for the physical."

"I'm fine."

"You are constantly whining this hurts, that hurts. You have enough pains to keep Bufferin in business for the next hundred years."

"Right now, the only pain I'm having is the one you're giving me in my ass."

"Go see your doctor. Get your physical. Maybe he can surgically separate you from the sofa."

"I'm fine."

She flapped her lips, wheeled around and headed toward somewhere in the back of the house. "Die early," she called back. "I don't care, the insurance is paid up, it's a payday for me."

Lloyd had wheezed his way through a few back-and-forth passes mowing the lawn before noticing his son sitting on the top porch step. Eddie's lips were moving but Lloyd couldn't hear him over the sound of the mower. He released the throttle bar, and the motor died. "Did you say something?"

"You're sweating so much you look like you've been out in the rain."

"It's hot."

"It's not *that* hot."

"Did you want something?"

"Well, it's just it's hot —"

"Didn't I just say that?"

"— and you look like you're suffering... I'm worried, you know, like, you keel over or something, it'd be nice someone is here."

"Your mother send you out here?"

"Dad, I care."

"How much do you want?"

"No, I'm serious. Especially since you had those pull-ups in your keyster."

"You mean polyps?"

"Whatever. Those things can, you know, kill you."

"Everybody gets polyps. It's no big deal."

"I worry, Dad. Can't I worry?"

"You're worried so much, *you* mow the lawn."

"That's not what I'm talking about."

"I know."

"Look, if it'll make you feel better, you go for the physical and I'll, you know, like, I'll drive you."

"How does that make me feel better? You've had your permit three days; you'll get us killed taking me for my physical. Wait a minute; is that what this is about? You get an excuse to take the Caddy out?"

"You know something, Dad? You got a bad attitude. You always think —"

"Ok, so let's say I say yes, I make the appointment, you get to drive me —"

"Great!"

"Hey, wait a second, I didn't say —"

Eddie was already halfway through the front door into the house. "I'm gonna call Julie."

"Who the hell is —"

"You don't mind she takes the ride with us, right?"

Julie came bouncing down the walk of her house in pink sneakers, stuck her metaled mouth in the passenger window and squeaked, "So you're Lloyd!"

"I'm Lloyd."

"Well, hello, Lloyd!" She had a ring in her nose, her hair cut into zebra stripes, and a ragged T-shirt with what looked like hand-painted scrawl reading, "Splatter Pattern Tour '17." According to the tour stops listed on the T-shirt, the Splatter Pattern Tour of 2017 evidently consisted of a single date at a local pizzeria/saloon. She bounced into the back seat, blew a kiss to Eddie and squeaked, "Let's see whatcha got Eee-dee." That's what she called Eddie: Eee-dee. Lloyd didn't know why.

Every time Eee-dee ran a stop sign, halted too far into an intersection, or drifted over the lane lines, Julie seemed to think it was pee-in-your-pants funny. She giggled a squeaky giggle, sometimes threw in a squeaky scream as she bounced around the back seat. "Jesus, Eee-dee, do you even know, like, what you're doing?"

Eddie would bobble his head, let his tongue loll out of his mouth, and jiggle the steering wheel spastically. "Duh, duh, maybe I don't, duh."

"Eddie don't horse around," Lloyd said, his right hand in a death grip on the arm rest.

"Whaddaya think, Jewels," Eddie said, doing his moron face in the rearview. "Think they should give me my license? Duh duh."

"Eddie! Watch the road!"

The car started to drift over the center line, a horn screamed, a driver screamed, and Eddie screamed, "Asshole!" as he yanked the car back on course. "What's his fucking problem?"

"Mouth, Eddie."

"Oh, Jeez!" Julie said. She was excited about something, and her squeaks jumped an octave making Lloyd wince. "Just imagine, like, you know, we get in an accident—"

I can easily imagine that, Lloyd thought.

"—and, like, we're all unconscious, you know? And our IDs are all messed up with, like, all the blood, right?

They're gonna think I'm with you! Like, I'm one of the family! Hey, Lloyd, want a daughter?"

"No."

"Oh, wow!" She was really enthused now, on a roll, in the sound range of a dentist's drill. "What if, like, oh *wow*, we all *died* together! And they bury me with you guys 'cause they think I'm, like, you know, your daughter and stuff! And then we're, like, you know, in another existence, like a Heaven only it's not Heaven, and 'cause I got, like, buried with you guys, over there in the other universe I *am* your daughter!"

She's right, thought Lloyd, that's not Heaven.

"Jules wants to be a writer," Eddie said as if that explained anything. "Well, not, like, books or stuff like that." Which did explain things for Lloyd. "You know, it's, what? Anime, right? Isn't that what you want to do, Jules? Write anime?"

"Miyazaki is, like, a *god!*"

Lloyd wasn't listening at that point. "Stop sign, Eddie, stop sign, stop sign *stop sign!*"

"Your blood pressure's up," Lloyd's doctor said, pumping the bulb for the b.p. cuff for a second reading.

"I can't imagine why," Lloyd said.

Lloyd's doctor frowned at the second result and unwrapped the cuff. "I don't like that. You know what you can do to help bring that down?"

"Move to Tahiti?"

"I'm not laughing, Lloyd," and the doctor gave Lloyd's belly a couple of pokes. "Thirty pounds. I'd settle for twenty, but thirty would be better."

Lloyd looked down at his doctor's belly. The shirt button over the doctor's navel was straining so tight, if it popped Lloyd knew it was perforate him completely, embedding itself in the wall behind him. According to the anatomical chart on the wall, Lloyd saw the trajectory would take the button through Lloyd's small intestine and rupture his appendix before it blasted out his back.

"How're your bowel movements?"

"My what?"

"When was the last time you had a movement?"

"A movement?"

"Alright, when was the last time you did a poop?"

"Now you're sounding kinda wussy."

"When was the last time you took a crap, ok? That better? The hell with it; I'm going to leave the name of a nutritionist at the front desk for you. Make sure you pick it up when you leave. Ok, now, I'm going to make you the best offer you've had all day: drop your pants and bend over."

Lloyd's doctor made the same joke every physical. It was never funny and sure as hell didn't make what was to follow any more pleasant.

Lloyd bent over the examining table, winced at the snap of rubber gloves, felt his whole body tighten at the sound of the rotating cap on a jar of Vaseline.

"Ready?"

"No."

"Hmph. Relax."

"I'm trying. What're you doing, digging for the Higgs Boson?"

"I'm impressed. What do you know about the Higgs Boson?"

"I know it's not up there."

"Those yours?" The nurse at the front desk nodded to Eddie and Julie pointing at the other patients in the waiting room and giggling.

"Depends," Lloyd said. "What'd they do?"

"Just remember to take them with you when you leave. Here's that nutritionist information and a referral."

Lloyd handed over his parking receipt. "Could you validate this for me?"

The nurse blinked. "Excuse me?"

"Could you validate my parking?"

"Somebody in the lot charged you for parking?"

"Were they not supposed to do that?"

The nurse turned to another nurse fiddling with files nearby. "Hey, Irma, I think ol' Bennie's at it again."

The second nurse asked Lloyd what the guy in the parking lot looked like.

"Old guy, only had about half his teeth, sitting on a little stool next to a sign that said, 'Parking, five dollars.'"

The nurses nodded. "That's Bennie."

"You're telling me he's not gonna be out there when I go out there."

"Doubtful," the one nurse said.

"Which means I'm not getting my five dollars back."

"Even more doubtful."

On the way out of the doctor's office, Lloyd conscientiously stuffed the nutritionist information, and the referral note and his useless parking ticket in a recycling bin, then took the car keys from Eddie saying the deal was for Eddie to drive him *to* the doctor. Lloyd would drive them home.

Eddie and Julie sat together in the back seat. Eddie went into a cartoony act of trying to look down the low collar of Julie's T-shirt. "Duh, duh, what the heck are those things?" Julie, squeaking like an unoiled bicycle, would bat at his hands, laughing.

"Really, Eddie?" Lloyd said. "You have to do that in front of me?"

"I'm just kidding, for God's sake, Dad. She knows I'm kidding, right, Jules?"

"Don't take it so serious, Lloyd," Julie said.

Jesus, the boy's a cunning little shit, Lloyd thought, with an equal mix of disgust and admiration. He pulls the semi-retarded just-fooling-around thing, but that still gets him a look at this girl's boobs.

"I'm gonna stop at the bakery," Lloyd said. "Get bread for dinner."

"Yeah, sure," Eddie said. *"Bread."* Then he whispered something to Julie and both started squeaking together.

Lloyd pulled up at the curb in front of the bakery and climbed out of the car.

"You didn't ask if we, like, wanted something?" Eddie asked.

"You can have anything you can pay for."

"Uh —"

"Bye."

As Lloyd stepped up to the counter, he could see through a doorway into the kitchen where a young girl was baking cookies, the big hand-sized ones. She was pulling a just-done tray out of the oven, and the aroma of those fresh-baked lovelies – chocolate chip it smelled like – filled the bakery. Lloyd could feel his mouth juicing up.

The counter woman stepped up to him and Lloyd ordered a loaf of French bread.

"Anything else?"

The fresh-baked-cookie smell was still heavy in the bakery, stewing up nicely with the smell of fresh bread and fresh cakes and fresh pastries.

"Um," Lloyd said. He was looking down at a tray of éclairs lined up like heart-killing torpedoes. They looked damn fine and Lloyd thought the day he'd had so far had earned him a treat.

The woman in the kitchen started buttering up the cookie tray for a second load. Watching the woman dip into a tub of butter reminded him of his doctor greasing up his rubber gloves.

Lloyd made a little grunting noise.

"I'm sorry," the counter woman said, leaning in. "Did you say something?"

Lloyd shook his head. "I'm good." He turned for the door and saw Eddie and Jules horsing around in the car, something that involved Eddie jumping back and forth over the front seat and Jules playfully yelling "Rape!" out the window. Lloyd had a brief vision of sneaking out the bakery's back door and walking home.

He reached for the loaf of French bread, then remembered Eddie liked chocolate chip cookies.

"Let me have one of those chocolate chip numbers, the big one there." Then he thought of Julie though it pained him to think of Julie and he said, "Better make it two."

He remembered Miriam liked the ones with almonds and vanilla chunks and he ordered one of those, too.

BRAD'S OFFICE

Brad was dead and I was going to get his office.

Jim, my boss, showed up at my door and said, "We should go have a look."

We walked across the floor to my new department. That's what this was about; I'd been promoted to manager, but I'd had to manage from the other side of the floor because there was no room for me where the department sat. But now Brad was dead. Actually, he'd been dead a while, but none of us knew what was "proper" about when to get this taken care of. We hadn't had to deal with this before.

Brad hadn't rated a manager's office. That's how we did things. Your rank determined the size of your office.

"But there's an open office right there!"

"Yeah, but that has five windows. That's a director's office. You're a manager. Managers only get three windows."

Brad hadn't rated a manager's office, or any kind of office, really. But the office and the job had been something of a gift. Brad had been on the staff of one of the eighth-floor execs, the big guys, but then he'd gotten sick. It became harder and harder for him to make it into the office, and hard for him to pull a full day when he did. Brad didn't want to just sit home and be sick. He wanted to keep working, so the company gave him the job on my floor because it wasn't very taxing, and he could do a lot of it from home. Then he was home more and more, then he wasn't coming in at all, and then the work stopped coming in, and then he died.

The company was still trying to figure out how to deal with this and they were having to deal with it more and more. This was the early days when, if you got that diagnosis, well, the general feeling was that was it. Maybe because we were in the entertainment business, it was hitting us particularly hard. Sometimes I wondered if banks and oil companies were going through what we did.

I knew Kermit; nice guy from down south somewhere. Him and his drawl had taught me how to use a desktop when the company bought our first generation of computers. He was gone.

John, the HR guy who decided how many windows you were allowed, he'd retired, suddenly, no preamble. The word was he was sick.

Tim down the hall was legendary for grabbing the guy most likely to be uncomfortable and whisking him out onto the dance floor at the Christmas party. It had become a company Yule time tradition. Tim was leaving to take care of his partner, and although nobody said it, we figured if his partner had it, Tim had it.

Again, maybe because we were in the entertainment business, a lot of us knew people on the outside, too. The girl I was seeing at the time, her cousin Brian was sick. He'd been an aspiring actor. Now he spent his time gathering and passing out information about possible untested, experimental, and "non-traditional" treatments. I remember there was one that had something to do with shark oil.

Jim and I walked across the floor, picking up Michael the intern on the way since he'd be working for me when I finally made the move. Jim opened the office door with the key HR had given him. Most of the department's staff were in cubicles along the hall. They looked up when they saw us at the office door, but they didn't say anything. I guess they'd had to figure that door was going to get opened eventually.

Inside, we were supposed to check the office out, see what needed to be done to get it ready for me, see if there was any personal stuff that had to be cleared out. Looked like anybody else's office: some posters on the walls, some videotapes and books on the bookshelves, photographs on the bulletin board over the desk. A lot of the photos were of Brad and different people; no repeats.

I didn't know Brad well; "Hello" in the halls, a few words when I'd had to drop stuff off for his boss on Eight, but I didn't remember him ever referring to having somebody. From the pictures, it didn't seem so. I asked Jim, but he didn't know.

I wondered if he'd had to go through everything alone. Brian hadn't had anybody, but his sisters and his mother in Maine would come down to see how he was doing. I'd heard his father hadn't spoken to him in years after he'd come out, but when he heard Brian was sick, and how sick he was, even he'd started coming down. I used to talk about that with my girlfriend, whether or not

Brian's dad was thinking about all that time he'd wasted not talking to his son. Looking at those pictures of Brad with different people, even though I didn't really know him I hoped there'd been somebody there for him. A partner, family, friends. Somebody.

There was a plastic medical waste container under the desk. Jim told us not to touch that; somebody with some kind of special designation had to take care of that.

We went through the desk drawers. Evidently, Brad had been a bit of a hoarder and a slob: a lot of pencil stubs, dirty worn-down erasers, pens, half-used Post-It pads, paper clips were jumbled together in one drawer in a mass a couple of inches deep. On top of the pile was an amateurishly printed flyer for some kind of weekend, the kind of weekend you didn't go on if you had someone. Jim and I agreed Brad's family didn't need to see that so I threw it out.

As we were going through Brad's desk, for some reason I remembered a story Jim had once told me about working for some city agency years before during one of the regularly occurring financial crises which had resulted in a hefty cut in the agency's budget. Jim said there'd been a table just inside the door where you came in in the morning; that's where the Facilities guys piled the disconnected phones of staffers who'd been hit in the layoff.

"When you came in in the morning," Jim had said, "the first thing you did was look to see if your phone was on the table. If it wasn't, you still had a job. If it was, you just turned around and went home."

Jim said sometimes he could recognize a phone; one with a smiley face sticker, another one with a pen holder still holding a pen with a hairy little troll on the end. He said that reminded him of his days as a Marine back in Vietnam.

Jim never told war stories about Vietnam. When *Platoon* had come out, I asked him if he was going to see it. "I just stopped having nightmares. Why would I go to see something that might start them again?"

But seeing the phones on that table, he said, brought back memories of a pile of helmets by a base hospital. They belonged to Marines who wouldn't need them anymore.

That all came back to me as we were going through Brad's office.

Jim had taken the photos off the bulletin board, said he'd get a phone number from HR, see if somebody wanted to pick them up or have us mail them. He said he'd take care of it and I was glad I wouldn't have to make that call.

Then we were done, and Jim and me and Michael stood there for a moment, looking around, a bit at a loss. Nobody knew the protocol.

Then Jim let out a little sigh and said, "What a fucking waste," and walked out.

Marine in Vietnam, the pile of helmets; if anybody could identify a fucking waste, I figured it was Jim.

A couple of weeks later, I was in the office. They had spackled over the holes in the walls where posters had hung and covered it all in bright, fresh paint, vacuumed the desk drawers clean, even refinished the desk. They always did that, so you could start fresh, like you were the first person to ever sit in that office.

In time, the faces on the floor changed, even Jim left, and there came a time when there was nobody left who remembered Brad had had that office before me. Then more time passed and I left. They would've spackled and repainted the office and refinished the desk again, and somebody new would sit there, and it would be like everything that had come before had never happened.

THE GENERAL

Sheri and I called him The General, this guy who used to walk his dog past our house every night. We had just moved in, were crashed out on the sofa, feet up on unpacked boxes, and we saw him go by the picture window.

"Ahh," Sheri said, "The General is inspecting the new troops!"

The guy was, I dunno, in his 50s, I'd guess, but trim, not an ounce of fat on him. And straight-spined, shoulders squared, head up. He had a majestic looking face, with big, bushy eyebrows, and a thick head of gray-streaked hair combed straight back.

He was wearing green work twills. I never found out what he did for a living, but they were always spotless and pressed. Between his at-attention bearing and those green twills and that walking-the-parade-ground pace, yeah, The General – it fit.

You would figure a guy like that would be walking something like a German Shepherd or a Doberman. But out in front of him at the end of six feet of leash was this little dust bunny of a dog, couldn't have been more than 10 inches high, probably didn't weigh more than a pair of work shoes. But it did walk like him; head up and proud, its little, pointed schnozz popping out of that fuzzball of a head, tail up like a pennant. You could barely see its little legs sticking out of all that fur, moving so fast to keep ahead of The General they were practically a blur, *bipbipbipbip*.

This was back when *The Jersey Shore* was big, so Sheri christened the dog Pouf because she said it looked like Snooki's pouf had escaped.

After a couple of nights we noticed The General and Pouf always passed by about the same time, around 7:10. They were so regular, sometimes we would bet the over/under: "A Burger King run says he runs late"; "He comes in early, you're going to Dairy Queen for me."

They may have been a mismatch, and that commanding face never showed anything, but I know

The General loved little Pouf. I was driving through the neighborhood one afternoon and I saw him sitting on the front porch of his house (kept as immaculate as his twills). I could hear the Mister Softee truck heading off down the street. The General sat with an ice cream cone for himself and held one down low for Pouf.

About a year after we moved in, we had little Neecy. My wife, who'd grown up with a dog, said *every* kid should grow up with a dog, so she found an ad online and we bought this thing that was part Bichon Frise, part who knows. It was small and cute, I guess, and friendly. Well, too friendly; Cotton (because she looked like a cotton ball as a pup) would go off with anybody who so much as gave her a wave.

I started passing The General on his nightly walk while I was walking Cotton. That was the first time I ever saw his face show anything: a smile. I think. It could've been just a twitch it was that small.

"I joined the club," I said, calling across the street.

He nodded, did his little twitch of a smile again, and walked on. The General approved.

We were in the house a couple of years when we noticed he and Pouf weren't keeping such great time anymore. They were passing the window later, and Pouf's little paws weren't *bipbipbip*-ing so fast.

"I guess Pouf is getting old," I said one night as they slow-marched past.

Sheri didn't say anything. She'd lived with a dog before; she already knew how that story always ended. I didn't figure it out until later.

And then they didn't pass by at all anymore.

"Maybe he just lets him out in the yard now," I said.

I was taking the garbage out one night, and Cotton sat on the porch watching because she thought every time I went out the door it was time for a walk. I got the cans to the curb, turned around, and there was The General. In his hand were several coils of leash with an empty collar hanging from the end.

I nodded a hello and then pointed to the leash. "Did he get away? I'll help you look for him."

"No," he said and then he didn't have to say anything more.

"Sorry."

He nodded. "I was going to put this out with the garbage. I thought...let me take the walk first."

Now that we had Cotton, I understood. I saw him look over at her, saw that little twitch of a smile.

"She recognizes you," I said. "Why don't you go say hello."

He looked unsure, so I gave him a nod to push him along. He sat on the top step and Cotton joined him. She didn't jump on him the way she usually did when someone showed an interest, but just leaned against him. The General ruffled her ears, then bent toward her. Cotton bowed her head, and he rubbed his forehead against hers.

The General stood, made a gesture at me with the coiled leash: thank you.

I nodded back: you're welcome.

Then he headed down the block and turned the corner on his way home.

GRACE NOTE

The truth of the matter was he really didn't think much of it when the girl went away. He was, naturally, a little sad, and he told her so, and they hugged and kissed and told each other how hard it would be to get through the weekend the way people who miss each other do. Still, he thought of it as more of a thing to do to impress the girl which it did.

Actually, he was worried that, perhaps, he had been spending too much time with the girl, thinking about the girl, and so on. He was, after all, a young fellow very used to spending most of his time by himself, enjoying himself however he could, and indulging in his own company. Now that she had come along, there was a part of him that was slightly jealous, slightly resentful of the time she was taking from him. So, maybe, he thought, he could take the weekend, these few days to himself, and enjoy himself, again, catch up on his reading, his thinking, catch up on his being alone again. He had spent a long time alone before her and had gotten very used to it. He was not so willing to completely let it go now. Perhaps the weekend would tell him. Perhaps the weekend would tell him many things.

But the small apartment that he called home seemed...somehow "off" when he got home that night. It had always been a quiet place, secluded, placed at an angle in the hall that he thought was enviably off the beaten track, isolated, but now it seemed more so, in some indefinable way emptier.

He shrugged off the feeling, kicking off his shoes, dropping his jacket across the back of a chair, there was no sense keeping the place neat just for himself. He made a sandwich for dinner, it didn't seem worthwhile to go through the bother of a hot meal, and plopped himself on the sofa, not worrying about the crumbs, his sandwich in one hand, a 7&7 in the other, the cold glow of the TV in front of him. He sighed contentedly. It had been a while since he'd spoiled himself like this, and it was nice not to worry about what the girl would think while she picked crumbs out from under the sofa cushion.

Nothing on the TV seemed very good, though, even the programs he usually liked. Maybe it was because they were re-runs, he thought, or they felt so tired and familiar they might just as well have been re-runs.

He finished the sandwich and slapped another one together, then mixed himself another drink. The liquor didn't seem to have the effect he thought it should have, that it used to have. The tingling taste was not there, that warm flow down his throat was not there, that relaxing, warming buoyancy was not there. And the drink, or something, seemed to be killing the taste of the food. The sandwiches were as tasteless as paper, no flavor, bringing no sense of being filled.

He couldn't help but notice that it seemed like he had an inordinate amount of time on his hands. He did not remember there ever having been so much time in a night. And there were other things he noticed that he did not remember ever having seen before. He did not remember the sofa as being so big, so full of empty space. He did not remember the way the shadows collected in the corners of his apartment. He did not remember his bed as being so empty, so uncomfortable, so inhospitable, the sheets being so cold when he climbed between them. He could not remember such an unpleasant, dreamless sleep, a sleep punctuated with early morning, restless ramblings around the apartment, another drink or two, a couple of unfulfilling bouts with late movies. He did not remember that a night could take so long to pass.

He awoke late in the day, nearer to the afternoon than the morning, still not rested and trying to shake the ill feeling of having had too much to drink the night before. It was a new day, and he tried to jump into it, willing to exercise his new, weekend freedom. He tried to read, watch a little TV, but his mind would not focus, not fix on the words before him, the images that offered themselves up.

But he would not allow himself to be depressed, however, and he took himself out for a walk around the neighborhood. All he needed, he assured himself, was to get out a little bit, some sunshine, some fresh air, and he went to bask in the small, green park on the cliffs overlooking the river. It was a bright, clear day, a day of crystal blue skies and puffy clouds, and many were in the park to enjoy the day: children, old folks, the not so old, and, lining the rails by the cliffs, the couples, young and old, newly formed and long established, gazing out at the glittering water occasionally cut by the plodding figure of a tug, a barge, a gliding yacht.

Somehow, the day was not as bright for him. He remembered spending a lot of time in the park, alone, while others held hands with their partners and looked at the world lit with a slightly different light. Odd, he thought, that he and the girl had spent a quiet day indoors together the previous weekend, weathering a dismal, rainy day watching old, boring movies on the TV and trying to make a meal of the odds and ends in his sparsely populated refrigerator, and yet he had felt much better that day than this, despite the rain, despite the old movies.

So, the walk did nothing for him, and he went back to his apartment and tried calling old friends, friends who had moved away, friends who had other business, friends who were no longer friends. He went out to the movies but did not remember much about the picture, and then he drank too much, again, and slept through another bad night.

He awoke Sunday more fatigued than the previous day, but also settled for the weekend had given him some answers.

One answer.

He spent the day cleaning the apartment, cleaning himself, and he vowed there would be no sign of the disarray that had marked the weekend, the confusion that had marred his apartment, that had marred him. And when, again, he saw the girl, they hugged and kissed warmly, and she inquired about his weekend

Of which he said little. He told her that he had caught up on his reading, his relaxing, that it was good to have some time alone to himself, again.

But he had eyes, and in his eyes, she could see, and so she knew, and in her eyes, he could see that she knew, and he decided that maybe that was not such a bad thing. That was, in fact, what it was all about.

THE DROWNED MAN

It was still dark when the first ferry of the morning pulled out. On the enclosed passenger deck over the well where a handful of cars were parked, Cy got a cup of foul-tasting black coffee at the snack bar and stood at one of the windows. He was alone on the deck; the handful of other early-morning passengers – must be commuters this early, he guessed – had stayed bundled up inside their cars. He could feel the vibration of the ferry's engines, sense more than feel the slight, queasy effect of the waves on the boat, but there was no sense of forward motion. Once the Cape May terminal had disappeared behind them, the ferry was a lone island of light suspended in a black void.

He threw the coffee away before it was half gone, stepped out onto the promenade, pulled the broad collar of his bridge coat up around his face, shelter against the stinging wind coming across the water. He flexed his fingers buried deep in his coat pockets, told himself the dull aches weren't age, that he'd grown stiff on the long drive, that it was, indeed, cold and anybody would've felt the same.

Even as he told himself this again and again, he knew none of it to be true.

After a while, he could see the lights of the ferry out of Lewes on the south side of the bay passing them by in the distance, the passing marking the halfway point of the trip.

The sky went from black to gray, an unbroken sheet of dour clouds, and below them, the waters of Delaware Bay turned a similarly cold, metallic colorlessness. In the distance, Cy could now see the shadows of large tankers anchored far out in the bay, each waiting its turn to come up the river to offload at the refineries near Philadelphia and Camden.

He had never liked being on big water. Whenever he found himself on open water a discomforting picture always appeared in his head. There he was, his little white body treading in place at the surface. Below him, quickly growing from a slight tint to utter blackness, were the deeps, unmeasured and immeasurable, a bottomless abyss so vast it could swallow anything mortal: a person, a ferry, a *Titanic*, Atlantis if you believed in that kind of thing; anything. And down there, hidden in the dark, things killed each other day in and day out. Your big fear was that — for no particularly good reason — one of those things might glance upward and see, way, way above, those two, pale flailing legs. Every summer a story came in from somewhere in the world proving that once in a while — for no particularly good reason — those things that lived down deep occasionally came to the surface for a kill. Out on the big water, you were not only vulnerable, you were also so god-awfully small. For no particularly good reason, you could get pulled under without leaving a ripple.

He found the garden apartment complex on the far side of Lewes. The buildings were laid out in lazy curls around frozen ponds and hillocks of wilted grass. There were little footbridges and plastic sunflowers with petals whirring in the wind.

He left his car in the lot, walked tiredly, his heavy-treading feet crunching on rock salt. He stopped on one of the footbridges and breathed deeply, clearing stale air from his lungs. He coughed, stretched, his head tilted back, looking up toward the gray-masked sky.

His cigarette case flashed silver even in the dull grayness. He lit a cigarette, the matching lighter also flashing, and when he was half-done, he tossed the glowing stub away, then found the door with her number, rang the buzzer.

"Who is it?"

He stood in front of the peephole. A chain rattled on the other side, the dead bolt slid clear, the door swung open.

"Hi, Tish."

"Cy..."

"Merry Christmas."

She was older, but her face had thinned nicely. Doing herself up in a different way: the brown hair – now with a wisp of gray – short, moving easily and casually, no longer cemented into a stiff, wiry nest. Make-up was relaxed, too: just a few, deft touches. Maybe she finally believed she was pretty.

She had her coat on, arms filled with papers, notebooks, a bulging briefcase of cracked leather. "I was just leaving."

"So I see."

"Are you all right?"

"Yeah, sure, just thought I'd drop in, you know, surprise you, seasons greetings sort of thing."

"You surprised me all right. Oh. I'm sorry. Come on in." She stood aside, letting him into the foyer, then closed the door after him. She looked at her watch.

"Work?" he asked. "What're you doing now?"

"I teach, Cy. I've been teaching for quite a while."

"You better go," he said. "I don't want you to be late." He reached for the door.

She put a hand out, holding it closed. "You look like hell."

"Just tired."

"Did you drive all night?"

He gave a meaningless non-answer of a shrug.

She took in the rumpled suit through his open coat, frowned at his red eyes and unshaven chin. "You shouldn't go back on the road in your shape. Why don't you crash here and get some rest? See what's in the fridge." Now she reached for the doorknob. "Help yourself. Clean up, get some sleep…"

"Good idea. Uh, where's the baby?"

"I switch off with a girlfriend, taking our kids to daycare. You missed her by about 15 minutes."

"Oh. Uh, Tish…I was sorry to hear. About Alan."

Her eyes flicked away, and she shrugged. She opened the door, and the cold came in.

"I guess I should've said something then," he said. He thought of telling her about his ride down for the funeral, sitting in his car at a distance, invisible.

She looked at her watch, again.

"You go, Tish," he said.

She started to leave but didn't. "You're *sure* everything's —"

"Fine. Positive. I just thought I'd pop in. Call it a holiday whim. What time'll you be back?"

She thought a moment. "There's a holiday assembly after classes today, then the faculty's supposed to — … I don't think until after six."

"This daycare place, they'll take care of her all that time?"

"My girlfriend'll pick her up and watch her until I come by. I'll try to get out early. See you about six."

She started down the walk. He stayed in the doorway and watched.

She turned back toward him. She was concerned which was nice to see. Less nice, he could also see she hadn't believed a word that had come out of his mouth. She walked to the parking lot and a small, brown Toyota as sensible as her shoes. When she'd driven off, he closed the door.

He drifted around the living room, to a small artificial Christmas tree on an end table, two dozen or so Christmas cards standing underneath including an enormous one of construction paper handmade by one of her classes, signed in different colored crayons with a splatter of barely legible names.

Along one wall, a put-it-together-yourself wall unit for the TV and some cheap stereo equipment. Framed photographs along the top shelf of the wall unit. Among them: Tish holding her daughter, still a soft and shapeless infant. Hugging Tish, a tall, lean man, gaunt face, hair a lifeless wisp, eyes – despite his smile – dull; the cancer already well into its work.

He poked around the kitchen, the kid's room, the bathroom, saving her bedroom for last. He flicked through her clothes in the closet, then went through her dresser. There was a strongbox tucked in the rear of the bottom drawer. It wasn't locked. Inside: a few hundred dollars in cash, insurance policies, pink slip for her car, official-looking documents from her school, birth certificates, a copy of her husband's death certificate and will and a will of her own, her divorce decree.

He picked up the wills, looked at Tish's, thought how odd it looked with this other last name. You should be used to that by now, he told himself. He didn't open it.

He picked up the divorce decree; didn't open that either. Even after twelve years, just holding it brought the letters clear into his head: SUPREME COURT OF THE STATE OF NEW YORK, KINGS COUNTY, Patricia Alice O'Brien Keely plaintiff against Cyril Michael Keely...

He couldn't remember what he'd done with his copy.

Patricia Alice O'Brien Keely *against* Cyril Michael Keely. That *against* always stung.

He put everything back in the box the way he'd found it, slid it back into place in the drawer.

He shook off his coat, sat on the unmade bed and started to take off his wingtips, smiled that they still carried some of the shine he'd gotten the morning before from the bootblack who worked his office floor, then stopped, picked up his coat and shuffled out to the living room. He hung his suit jacket over the back of a chair, bundled up his coat at one end of the sofa. He pulled off his shoes, stretched out on the cushions, lay his head on his bundled coat.

He was asleep before his eyes finished closing.

Cy heard the front door open. "In here."

He set down the spatula, turned, she was in the kitchen doorway. Her hand swallowed the hand of a slightly bigger, more defined version of the little girl he'd seen in the photos in the living room. The girl had Tish's straight, loose brown hair, small, pug nose, full-lipped mouth now pursed into a puzzled pout. But he didn't know the eyes: wide, curious, a burning ice blue.

"Hello," Cy said.

The little girl took a step back from the new face, tucking herself behind her mother's coat.

"This is my friend I told you was visiting," her mother said. "Say hello."

The girl shuffled across the kitchen flat-footedly, held out a splayed hand which she seemed ready to pull back at the slightest perceived threat. "Hi."

Cy took the offered hand gingerly. "Hi yourself."

"I'm Mithelle."

"Hi, Michelle. I'm Cy."

"Is it ok if Cy has dinner with us?" Tish asked.

The little girl shrugged, pulling her hand back, not at all enthusiastic at the prospect.

"Ok. Go hang up your coat and wash your hands."

The girl shuffled out slowly, stopping to look back over her shoulder for a last, studying look at Cy.

Cy felt better after she was out of the room and her little cold eyes were off him. "'A friend of Mommy's'?"

"Feel free to explain it all to her."

"Maybe in a few years. How old did you say she is?"

"I didn't." Tish shrugged off her coat and went into the living room. "She'll turn four in February."

"She looks bigger than her pictures."

"They're old pictures. I stopped taking them after Alan died. I don't know why." She hung up her coat and dropped on the sofa near where she'd set her briefcase and papers.

"You should take new ones," he said.

She kicked off her sensible shoes and rubbed the soles of her feet on the rug. "I can't believe you still have the Buick. I saw it in the parking lot. It staggers the imagination that it still runs!"

"It runs. Remember when we took it up to Lake George for our first anniversary? I always thought of that trip as our *real* honeymoon."

"We had a honeymoon, Cy."

"We had a weekend at the Plaza and then that Monday I was back at work. That wasn't much of a honeymoon."

"I liked it."

"So did I. It's just... Well..." He shrugged, not really sure what he was trying to say.

"Hm. Table's set," she noted, "dinner's on the stove..."

"I was thinking of answering the door wearing nothing but Saran wrap. I read where husbands like that kind of thing."

"That could've put me off dinner. What smells so fattening? Is that garlic bread I smell?"

"Oh, crap..." He ran back to the kitchen, grabbed a potholder and pulled a tray of slightly charred garlic bread from the oven.

"Mmmm." She was behind him, looking over the pots on the stove. "Garlic bread, linguini, white clam sauce... You've been doing some shopping."

"Kept me busy. I didn't know what you were eating these days."

"I'm trying to lose weight. I'm *always* trying to lose weight."

"It shows. I mean you look good, Tish. You look nice."

"Thank you."

"I noticed from the fridge you're trying to be careful, so I bought this special protein pasta or whatever the hell it's called. It's got added something. Supposed to be healthy, I guess."

"Very considerate. Very commendable. Well…"

They'd run out of things to say.

"Why don't I call you when it's ready?" he said.

"Good. I've got papers to mark, so…"

"Perfect. You do that, and I'll let you know when it's up."

She went back to the living room and turned the stereo on, some easy listening goop. He heard the shuffle of papers.

When dinner was ready, Tish put Michelle on a booster seat and they all sat to eat in the dining area.

Tish asked the girl about her day, but Michelle's answers were mumbled and monosyllabic, her wide, curious eyes always returning to study Cy.

"Maybe she's shy," Cy said, although he didn't feel like she was shy. The feeling he got from those eyes was, Who the hell are *you*?

"Usually, I can't shut her up," Tish said. "Are you feeling ok, Hon?" She laid the back of her hand on the girl's forehead. "So, Cy, how's the job? If I remember right, shouldn't you be coming up on your twentieth?"

"Next month. Actually...I'm leaving."

"Really?"

"You seem surprised."

"I am. I mean, when we were —" She cut herself off, careful now about what she said in front of her daughter. "You used to talk about doing something else, but... I'd gotten to thinking you'd never really leave."

"Next month, I'm gone."

She caught something...in his voice? His face? He studied his plate.

"Where you goin'?" Michelle asked, but it didn't sound like curiosity to Cy, not with the stare behind it.

"I'm retiring from my job," Cy said and put on a smile.

Michelle nodded, moving her fork through her linguini without eating any, keeping her eyes on Cy.

"Is it a retirement, Cy?" Tish asked. But he knew she knew.

He gave a sighing smile, a little embarrassed at being caught out. "Sort of. It's been suggested I 'seek out other opportunities.' I knew it was coming. You look around and you're the oldest person in your department, your boss is younger than you, *his* boss is younger than you, you kind of know..."

She nodded.

"It's fine, though. I'm ok. I've done well. I don't even have to work if I don't want to. But I've been talking to some people, looking at a few things. Maybe I'll finally get around to doing those other things I was always talking about."

"You should." Then she grinned. "Maybe you could celebrate your new-found freedom by getting a new car."

"Wazza matter with your car?" Michelle asked.

"He just has a really old car," Tish said. "So, when did all this happen?"

"It happened," Cy said, trying to make it look unimportant with a pointless little smile and an equally meaningless shrug. That was more comfortable than saying, Close of business yesterday in a quick conversation with my director, followed by some brooding drinks at a bar, then some brooding hours in my apartment, then climbing in my car in the middle of the night to head south.

"How about you?" Cy asked. "How's your job?"

"Long hours, short money, but I like it. You know how that goes. Alan left us pretty well fixed. I'm like you; I don't even have to work. But…" She paused, trying to figure out how to express it. "I always had my teaching certificate."

"I remember."

"I never used it. I thought it was my job to be your —" a quick concerned look to the little girl " – to be a wife; that's all."

Michelle was looking from Cy to Tish, and Cy could tell the girl was trying to decode what wasn't getting said.

"I'm sorry —"

Tish waved it away. "It wasn't…all on one side. Well, not entirely. That's what I thought I was supposed to do. I like what I do now. I like that I'm *doing* something. Oh, the kids are often a pain in the ass —"

"Mom!" Michelle barked.

"I'm sorry, Hon," Tish said to her daughter. "You're right. Mommy used a bad word." She smiled at Tish, proud of her daughter, proud of the power her daughter had over her. "As I was saying, the kids can be a pain *in the neck* –" she looked over to Michelle, waiting for her approving nod " – and their parents are worse, and there's as much political backbiting and bureaucratic b.s. –" a quick glance at Michelle to see if "b.s." passed muster " – as you ever saw at your office. But there are days when you connect with the kids and…" She didn't know how to finish it, but Cy nodded, pretending to understand.

"I saw the Christmas card they made."

She beamed and dug into her linguini. "Home-cooked meal like this is a treat. I don't usually have time to make something decent. Even when I have a little time…" She flapped her lips tiredly. "I almost didn't get our Christmas tree. We didn't have one last year. Or the year before. You know…"

"I know."

"I wanted to have one this year. For my princess." She smiled, leaned over and ruffled the girl's hair.

Michelle shrugged the hand off, embarrassed in front of Cy.

"Seeing anybody?" He thought he'd managed to make it sound casual.

"Not really. I mean, I go out once in a while, but…"

"Yeah."

"It's hard right now. I know it's been a while, but sometimes it doesn't feel that long."

"Sure."

"And you?"

He twirled some linguini thoughtfully on his fork. Not enough garlic, he thought. "About the same."

The little girl dropped her fork in her plate with a heavy clink and let out a very theatrical, very bored sigh.

"You want to go watch TV?" Tish asked and let her go.

Then Tish was clattering around in the kitchen, cleaning up, Cy was slouched on the sofa, and there was something warming against the cold night in the familiarity of that.

The little girl had her chubby fingers clamped around the TV remote. She kept stabbing the channel selector button, flicking between several channels running cartoons. She looked over at him; he smiled, pretending the constant flicking didn't annoy the hell out of him.

When Tish finished in the kitchen, she came into the living room and put the little girl on her lap. They watched *Rudolph the Red-Nosed Reindeer*. The mother and daughter chatted and giggled at the Claymation reindeer and his luminescent nose, and an odd elf that wanted to be a dentist, and a prospector looking for a peppermint mine. The little girl forgot about the man on the sofa. Her mother seemed to forget about him, too.

"Thanny Clauth!" Michelle called out, beaming and pointing at the ho-ho-ho-ing Claymation figure on the screen.

"That's right! Santa Claus! And he'll be here in just a few days!" Tish tickled Michelle's small, round belly. The girl tried to tickle her back.

"Ith a cow!" Michelle pointed at the reindeer.

"No! That's a reindeer, silly!"

"Ith a *cow!*" Michelle thought this was a funny joke.

"Reindeer, you silly magilly!" Tish tickled her, again.

"*Cow!*" Michelle laughed.

Cy turned to the window behind him.

After Rudolph led Santa off around the world, Tish took Michelle by the hand and brought her over to Cy. "Say goodnight to our guest."

"G'nigh'."

Cy put on a small smile. "Good night."

Michelle looked over her shoulder at him as Tish led her out, those blue eyes still cold, cautious, studying. Cy turned away, toward the TV.

After they left the room, he turned the set off, listened to the night's routine. Water ran in the bathroom, dresser drawers shuffled. There were some giggles, the boinging of bed springs, a few rhyming couplets of Dr. Seuss, whispered goodnights, the quiet smack of a kiss.

He turned on the stereo, twirled the dial until he found something quiet and easy.

When Tish came back, she was wearing a bulky, shapeless robe over baggy pajamas. She got something from the kitchen.

"Remember this?" he said and pointed to the stereo: James Taylor singing "Fire and Rain." "I took you to see him. It was our first Valentine's Day. He was great, wasn't he? It was over in Jersey somewhere. Not the arena; he's not an arena kind of act. It was somewhere down the Parkway, wasn't it? Down around — ..."

She turned off the radio, smiled, then, an odd twist of her lips, not nostalgic, not...not anything he could read. She dropped tiredly into the easy chair; legs tucked neatly under herself. She began spooning something out of the little jar she'd brought with her from the kitchen.

"What's that?" he asked.

"Dessert."

"What happened to your diet?"

"It's baby custard."

"I saw it in the fridge. I thought it was for the kid."

"She's a little old for baby food, Cy."

"So are you."

"True. Would you like some tea?"

"Coffee?"

"I don't keep coffee. I have some herbal tea. Don't make a face. Try it."

"No, thank you."

"It keeps you regular," she grinned.

"Not a problem here. I, um, meant to tell you, to call..."

She waited.

"You know, to say how sorry I was about —"

"You said that this morning." She looked into her jar of baby custard. "I appreciate your saying it."

"How old was Michelle?"

"She'd just started walking. She won't remember him. I have pictures, I'll tell her stories, but she was too young. There won't be anything for her to hold on to. It's sad, but…" She shrugged, resigned. "I don't know. Maybe it's better that way. She won't miss him." She dropped the spoon into the empty jar, set it on the coffee table. "What I like about teaching is I have her all the time in the summer."

"You took a chance having her… You know, because, well…"

"Because of my 'advanced years'?"

He shrugged, a little embarrassed. "I don't know I'd have said it like that."

Her eyes dropped into her lap. "Alan was already sick. We thought — … We both thought there should be something…for after…" She shook her head, laughing at herself. "I don't know how to explain it without sounding silly."

"I miss you." It surprised him to realize he'd said it aloud. "It was no whim, me coming here."

"Really?" she asked, smirking. "Honest?"

"Don't make fun. I wanted to see you again."

She studied him. "What happened?   Is this about the job?"

Yes, it was about the job, and yes, he had been seeing someone, there'd been several someones, and it was about all that and a hundred other things, too.

"No, it's not," she said, answering her own question, then she nodded and seemed to understand what even he didn't quite understand.

"I mean this as a compliment and I hope you take it that way," he said, "You're more astute than you used to be."

"I teach kids, Cy. They're worse than any of those hungry junior execs at your outfit. If you're not sharp, they'll eat you alive."

They both laughed and he was glad because he needed a laugh just then.

"There's nothing here, Cy. There's nothing left."

"That's a little too pat."

She shrugged: tough.

He was dying for a cigarette, but he figured you didn't smoke in an herbal tea home.

He turned his head to the misted window glass. He rubbed a peephole with his knuckle. The grounds were covered with a thin layer of frost. The world was empty, quiet, lit by cold fluorescents along the walks and Christmas lights flashing red, green, yellow and blue in apartment windows. "Do you remember our first Christmas?"

"After all this time – years, Cy — you didn't honestly expect there'd still be something, did you?" she asked.

He kept looking out the window.

"I'm sorry, then," she said.

"There's nothing to be sorry for."

"I failed you, Cy. You don't have to be nice about it. I did. I could make excuses. I was young. We both were. But I'm not sure excuses matter now. If it was today, maybe it'd come out differently. But it didn't happen today. It was a long time ago."

"I'll leave in the morning if that's all right."

"Fine." She stood. "You know, you really should get rid of that car."

He looked at her in her frumpy pajamas and frumpy bathrobe standing in the small living room of her messy, little apartment and he could see just how much time had passed, how long gone what had been between them was.

"Good night, Cy."

He raised a hand, heard her bedroom door close.

He put the empty jar of baby custard in the kitchen sink, turned off the apartment lights, stretched out on the sofa, massaging his knuckles, feeling a slight arthritic heat under his hand. He could hear her climb into bed and slip under the covers, the click of her night table light.

She didn't need him. She didn't *need* anybody. This was her place, her life.

It came to him he didn't really know her anymore.

The windows over the sofa where Cy lay were filled with the yellow light of morning and it felt good and warming on his face. He sat up on the sofa, stretched.

The apartment was quiet. Tish and the little girl were gone. That's best, he thought.

He pulled on his wingtips, shook out his suit jacket and slipped it on, and did the same for his bridge coat.

She'd left coffee on the stove, but he didn't bother. He pulled on his jacket, stood in the front doorway looking around the apartment for a long moment. No sign he'd ever been there.

You go under and you don't even leave a ripple.

TIDES

The red and blue and white lights from the wheels and coasters play on the black water as it rolls inshore past the pilings. In the dark, from a distance, the rides all look like pieces of the same machine: a moving, glittering Rube Goldberg contraption producing shrieks and laughter and music.

The pier looks just as bright and loud forty years ago, but back then, I never looked at it from a distance. Back then, I was always inside the machine. Every kid I knew spent time in the machine.

It's that time when we're all out there on the dusky streets, dog tugging at the end of a leash in one hand, a poop bag rustling in the other. I see him across the street, big guy, big hands, arms filling his sleeves to bursting, still in dusty work twills and muddy Frankenstein work boots. At the end of his leash, a little white-and-black fluff leading him, showing him when to stop, then waiting for him to grunt down in a tired squat to pick up the mess.

He sees me looking, he smiles, I smile – we're in the same union, brother – and we each walk on.

On Sundays, I always stop by the lottery counter before doing the groceries. Sometimes Cat is with me. When she is, I say, "For luck," and she kisses my new tickets.

She kisses them a little peck, but it's not for luck I think. That little half-pucker is like what she used to do as a baby just learning to kiss. It's not for luck. I like to think it's for me.

We don't win, we never win, but that's ok. It's something we do.

"I've been thinking," her mother says.

Whenever she says something like that – "I have an idea," "You know what might be nice? Might be fun?" – the hair on my neck goes up. Whatever it is, it's something I'm not going to think is nice or fun or a good idea.

"We should do something *special* for our next vacation."

Yep, there it is, right there in the way she hit *special*.

At that point, I know I'm supposed to express some interest, some eager curiosity. Any other option would only put off the inevitable. But if all I can buy is a 20-minute reprieve, I'm going to take it.

"Hold that thought, sweetie," I say, and gave her a quick kiss on top of her head as I pass. "I think the dog has to go out."

The coaster, they called it the Wild Mouse when I was a kid, I only rode it then and haven't been on it since. Later, it was the Jet Star but it was the same thing. Now, it's debris. Some latticework and a piece of rail out in the surf. The rest – the pier, the boardwalk, the big machine once filled with shrieking kids – out there in the ocean somewhere.

A piece of me washed out to sea with it.

PEONIES AND CIGARS

"Moms," R.J. pronounced, "do not date."

It was a pizza and beer place not far from the campus where they usually wound up in the evenings to share thoughts on life, love, and flunking out over a pie and pitcher of beer or three.

"Moms are people, too," Paulie C. said. Paulie C. was pre-law. Wussy cracks like that, R.J. thought, means a definite future public defender.

R.J. rebutted appropriately with a long, wet raspberry.

"You want she should be a nun?" Paulie Q. said. "How long's it been? I mean, you know, your dad and all. I mean, you know, with respect."

"Not the point," R.J. said, pouring himself another mug. "Point is she's a mom. That's just something moms don't do. They're *moms*, for Chrissakes."

"I think it's you're a bigot," Paulie C. said.

"You're calling *me* a bigot?"

"I'm just saying."

"Who dated that Shauna girl?" R.J. said.

"Well, let's face it," Paulie C. said, "she was *hot*."

"She *was* hot," Paulie Q. said. "But, c'mon, ya gotta give it to him, she was black."

"Yeah, but she wasn't *black* black. She was Halle Berry black. When you're Halle Berry black, you're not black; you're *hot*."

"How come you can be that stupid and not be flunking out?" R.J. said.

"I'm just saying," Paulie C. said.

"He's not giving you proper credit," Paulie Q. said.

"Thank you," R.J. said.

"But Shauna *was* hot."

R.J. blew him a raspberry, too.

In point of fact, R.J. didn't know how black Clarence was when his mom had first told him about meeting the man, although he was pretty sure the Halle Berry standard wasn't going to apply. R.J.'s head was still reeling over the idea his mom was seeing *anybody* let alone a black man when his mom emailed him some pictures from an afternoon in the park she'd had with Clarence. It turned out Clarence was *really* black, not so much because he was *black* black – meaning very dark in complexion – but because he looked very much like a black man. Until then, R.J. hadn't realized he'd been hoping for something in the Will Smith mold; someone who didn't come off so *terribly* black...

At which point he began asking himself about the same point Paulie C. had brought up; did this mean he was prejudiced? Or just *somewhat* prejudiced? And wasn't *everybody* just a *little* prejudiced?

That was the kind of mental merry-go-round that gave him a headache. He found it was easier to get his head around the simpler idea that his mom was a mom, and moms don't date.

In a series of calls badgering R.J. to come home and meet mom's new beau (which she said with a giggle that made R.J. pretend to gag even when there was no one to witness his performance), he'd learned that Clarence was a landscaper, that he took care of all the flowers and shrubs in the open air mall in Cape May where his mom worked in a homemade chocolate shop, and that he was "a really, really nice guy; I mean *really* nice," which, Ronnie thought, didn't make him any less black or make the idea of his mom dating any less weird. He was happy he was at NYU, his mom and Clarence were at the far end of Jersey, and he and the weirdness need never meet.

Ronnie knew immediately who the man sunk in one of the sagging sofas in the lobby of his dorm was. He was shaped like a beer keg, short and round, his close-cropped, kinky hair dusted lightly with grey, and he was *really* black. He had an unlit cigar (no smoking in the lobby) parked in the corner of his wide, downturned mouth.

As soon as Ronnie came through the door, the man struggled to get out of the marshy sofa. "Ronnie."

R.J. nodded. Even though he knew who the man was, he'd put off his mom so many times about meeting Clarence that Clarence had become a bit abstract to him; like a point you could argue passionately about in Poli Sci even though it didn't really matter a damn to how you got through your days. But here he was, in all his pudgy, black flesh; real.

"I'm Clarence."

R.J. nodded again.

"There some place we can get a beer?" Clarence said.

R.J. started to lead Clarence toward his beer and pizza place but then figured he didn't need the headache of bumping into the Paulies. There was a small neighborhood bar a few blocks from the dorm, a lot of older types playing older songs on the jukebox while they watched whatever game was in season on the TV over the bar.

Clarence dropped some change in the juke, played some Four Seasons and Smokey Robinson, ordered a couple of Shaefers, then they found a booth along the back wall.

"I thought we oughta meet," Clarence said around his cigar. He'd lit it up on the walk over, automatically put it out when they got to the bar, but left it planted in one side of his mouth. R.J. wondered if he ever took it out, if he faced his mom with that thing pointing at her. "Your momma calls you R.J. That what you like to be called? You got a preference?"

R.J. didn't like the way he said "momma." That seemed a black thing to him; didn't fit with his mom. "R.J.'s fine."

"I thought we oughta meet 'cause —" Clarence stopped, squinted his already squinty little eyes at R.J. "Did she tell you the news?"

A cold lump in his stomach and a hot flash on his neck told R.J. he probably already knew what the news was going to be. He only managed to shake his head.

"Well, looks like we're engaged. You know; to be married."

"Oh." It came out more like a squeak than R.J. would've wanted.

"So, you can see why I thought maybe we should finally, you know...meet."

R.J. nodded.

"It's gotta be hard when somebody like your momma decides to get married again. Harder when she marries somebody like me."

R.J. tried to produce a nonchalant shrug like none of that was a big deal to him but was pretty sure it only conveyed the opposite.

Clarence smiled, and the smile said, I don't believe you but I'm too polite to say anything more than what he did say which was, "Ok."

They sat there quietly for a bit, sipped their beer for lack of anything better to do, tossed a glance or two at the TV and shrugged judgmentally at whatever was going on in whatever game it was they weren't following.

"So," Clarence finally said.

R.J. realized Clarence was tossing the ball to him.

"Look," R.J. said after another quiet bit, "if she's happy, I'm happy."

Clarence smiled, truly amused this time. "That's one way of saying just about nothing."

And knowing that was true, R.J. had to smile, too. "I was surprised she was even *dating* anybody."

"And then it's...me."

R.J. nodded.

"And now the marriage thing."

R.J. nodded, again.

Clarence laughed. He had a deep, round laugh, although it had a nice, soft quality to it, muffled inside that beer keg chest of his. "You know that mall where your momma works? So, the town hired me to do up something in this new set of planters they put in. Your momma, I guess she was on her break or something, I look up and she's laid out on this bench, resting her feet. Tell you the truth, boy, I don't know who said what to who first. I really don't remember. All I know is first we're talking, then we're having lunch..." Clarence shrugged as if how things had gotten from there to here was as much a puzzle to him as to R.J.

"Not much of a love story," R.J. said.

"I'm 59, boy. Love stories aren't as hot and steamy at 59 as they used to be."

For the first time, R.J. laughed, and Clarence laughed with him.

They chatted. Clarence was originally from Baltimore and had had a decent landscaping business down there until his wife died of cancer four years ago. His brother had had another landscaping outfit in North Wildwood, not far from Cape May, and when the brother had had a heart attack, he'd asked Clarence to come in with him and now Clarence was pretty much running the show.

"I'll be 60 in a couple months, boy," Clarence said, "I'm carrying too many pounds, I shouldn't be smoking these damn things. I don't think I've got a whole lotta years to go. But I like your momma, and she seems to like me. I didn't come up here to ask your permission, or to even like me. But you're her son and I thought we should meet. I'm not out to be your new daddy or anything. You're grown up; you don't need *anybody* to daddy you. But I want your momma to be ok with this, too." Clarence took another pull on his beer. "Now, half your relatives stopped talking to her when your daddy died, and the rest stopped talking to her when they found out about me. It's no different on my side, and I got two daughters I'm not sure'll ever even say boo to me again. You understand what I'm trying to say here?"

R.J. studied his fingertip running round one of the wet circles left by his mug on the tabletop. "Serious, now; is my mom happy?"

Clarence looked puzzled. "Happy? *Your* momma? The Crab Queen of Cape May?"

They both laughed, then, because somehow, they both knew that whatever was going on between Clarence and his mom was real and solid, and not some weird, flingish thing.

R.J. called for two more Shaefers and raised his fresh glass. "Let's leave it at this. I'll come to the wedding, and we'll take it from there."

Clarence touched his glass to R.J.'s with a gentle clink.

When R.J. got down to Cape May the day before the wedding, a cab let him off at the house and there was Clarence, on his hands and knees in front of his mom's boxy little Cape Cod. Clarence was wearing coveralls and a frayed-brimmed straw hat, work gloves, and his cigar. He was poking around some peonies with a trowel.

"I wanted the house to look nice for the wedding," Clarence said.

R.J. knew things would be all right, then.

10-11

Hanratty turned the squad car onto the narrow side street the same way he did everything; with an absolute minimum of effort. He moved the wheel one-handed, shuffling it by under the bulge of his middle-aged, 20-years-of-eating-fast-food-on-the-run gut. The squad didn't turn smoothly; it wavered a little left and right, unsure under Hanratty's lazy-ass, one-handed helmsmanship, and Manny's face tightened in a wince, sure the cruiser was going to bounce off the cars squeezed in bumper-to-bumper at either curb.

Manny hated riding with Hanratty. Everybody hated riding with Hanratty. They'd hated riding with him long before he put in his papers, but with just a few weeks left on the job, he was an even bigger pain in the ass then he'd been before. He'd been going up to the watch commander after every roll call to bluntly declare that with his days on the job numbered in low double-digits, no way was he risking a busted nose, bruised knuckles, or thrown-out back – let alone something maybe lethal – so think twice about what calls were sent his way, and if he had a problem with that, the watch commander could fuck himself and take it up with his PBA rep.

But Manny was new to the house, and he was a probie, which meant he was double-fucked in that on either point his vote didn't count, so he was stuck with Hanratty and getting what seemed like every flyweight bullshit are-you-fucking-kidding-me call on their side of town.

Which – and Manny figured this was no coincidence – was the shitty side of town, and that was saying something in a town where even the good side was the good side because it was only moderately less shitty than the shitty side.

They were on a 10-11 which Manny had never heard called before, and when he'd asked Hanratty what the code meant – "Oh, I forgot; you're fuckin' retarded" – he learned that the only thing he was going to learn from

Hanratty was that he wasn't going to learn anything from Hanratty except how to be a prick. After a bit, Hanratty sighed an ok-I'll-do-you-this-one-favor sigh and said with barely moving lips, "Dog case."

The street jinked onto an even narrower passage that must've been one of the oldest pieces of road in town; still had bricktop, rumbling under their tires, setting the squad rocking on its blown-out shocks. The street was lined with century-old tenements, their windows broken or boarded up, the years of built-up soot on their faces tiger striped by old rains. The ground floors had been stores, their front windows painted over with soap or black paint or covered with rusted security gates or graffiti-covered steel rolling doors. Manny could see a few blocks down to where there were no buildings, just cleared lots that were supposed to be where the city was going to try to rebuild itself except it'd run out of money even before it'd finishing knocking down the derelicts. Now, that open ground was a dump for everything from household trash to busted-out furniture, bald tires, junked cars, mold-streaked refrigerators and anything else not worth keeping or stealing.

The curbs were clear down here because only someone psychotically optimistic would ever park their car here thinking it wouldn't get trashed, stripped, or stolen. Hanratty pulled the squad up behind a row of official-looking vehicles parked in front of a place with an unlit neon sign that said "Willy's." The sign had a neon picture of a martini glass with bubbles floating out of it even though martinis don't bubble. The squad's right-hand tires made a painful chirp as Hanratty ran them up against the curb.

"Nicely done," Manny said.

"How'd you like a 9 mm through your fuckin' left eye."

Manny quietly humphed.

With the slightest of motions, Hanratty pointed his veined, jelly-globed face toward the radio which was his minimalist way of telling Manny it was his job to call in that they were on scene.

There was a crowd of black and Hispanic faces gathered across the street from Willy's.

"One a these fucks makes a Ferguson crack 'n' you're gonna see me on the news tonight," Hanratty said. "Put a nine through his fuckin' left eye."

Manny wondered where they'd come from since there wasn't a legit residence for blocks around. The December wind funneling down the street was filled with needles but still didn't dissuade the lookers-on from thinking there was something to look on at, but it did dissuade Hanratty from getting out of the car. He nodded – another barely perceptible motion — at the knot of guys huddled in the front doorway of Willy's and said, "Ok, Pedro, go see."

Manny twitched a bit at the "Pedro," zipped up his jacket, pulled up the bogus fur collar, tugged on his gloves, then climbed out, setting his arctic cap on his head.

Years ago – a lot of years ago – Willy's had probably been one of those cozy neighborhood bars, the kind Manny remembered his dad stopping in for a shot and a beer on his way home, maybe watch an inning or two of a ball game on the TV before he headed out, always with the same faces sitting at the bar. Somehow Willy's had managed to limp along even as the neighborhood around it was dying and getting razed, until it couldn't limp any further which was why there was a city seal across the double doors and a car from the constable's office, a station wagon from the Board of Health, a car from the ASPCA, and a van from Animal Control parked at the curb.

There was another set of wheels there, too, a van with an illustration on the side panel of a fierce-looking German shepherd wearing a sheriff's badge and a snarl and wielding a huge medieval mace. "Mace K-9 Security" was spelled out in red, Gothic letters above the picture.

The respective drivers of these vehicles were trying to squeeze inside the archway framing the bar's double doors to get out of that cut-to-the-bone wind. Manny joined them, there was some handshaking and introductions.

"Love one another, brother!" somebody from the crowd across the street called out.

"Where do these people come from?" The constable was a young guy in a nice, tailored bridge coat. He kept eyeing the crowd and nibbling his trim mustache. "I swear, it's always the same people. I swear, they drive around all day looking for something to gawk at."

The guy from the Board of Health was a young, serious black gentleman with an overabundance of forehead and steel-rimmed glasses that made him look even more serious. He started giving Manny, in more detail than Manny could digest, the myriad difficulties Willy's had had with the Board of Health, the Bureau of

Consumer Affairs, the Liquor Authority, and the Bureau of Taxation. The upshot was that the city had seized the pub, and the owners had subsequently disappeared. "Only they didn't bother to tell anybody about the dogs," the Board of Health said. He said it with a bit of a bite to it, giving the constable a nasty look at the same time.

"We didn't think the dogs were still in there," the constable answered with his own bit of bite. "We assumed the owners would've come for the dogs."

"You assumed wrong."

"That better be a collective 'you,' pal."

Manny faded out on the debate, turning to another member of the conclave, a kid in green overalls who didn't look old enough to drive. "I guess you're the dog catcher?"

The kid wiped a gloved hand past his runny nose. "Something wrong with that?"

"No, I —"

"It's not like the cartoons, ya know."

"Yeah, I —"

"I mean, we don't run around in white coats with butterfly nets, ya know."

"I didn't —"

"We got radios, homing devices, tranquilizer darts, it's all real scientific, ya know."

The kid was with a weedy fellow whose long, scraggly hair seemed twenty years out of step with all the gray in it. He was from the ASPCA. "I think he's got the point, Albert," he told the kid.

By then the business between the Board of Health and the constable was getting a bit heated, so Manny gave them a calm-down wave. "Save it for the budget meetings, guys, ok?"

"Throw a penalty flag on 'em, ref!" somebody from the crowd yelled out.

"I swear, where the hell do these people come from?" the constable said.

"Now what's with these dogs?" Manny asked. "What do you mean there's dogs in there? What're they doing with dogs?"

"Watch dogs," the Board of Health said.

"For what?" Manny said. "Look at this dump. What'd they have anybody wanted to steal?"

"They'd steal the hinges off the doors just to do it," the constable said. "I'm surprised they haven't."

Manny turned to the one guy who hadn't introduced himself. "Didn't you guys notice you were short a couple dogs?"

"Hey, buddy, you know how many dogs we got in our kennels?" The representative of the Mace K-9 Security Service was crew-cutted, beer-bellied, and hunched down deep in his red plaid lumberman's jacket. Manny caught a glimpse of some kind of snaky tattoo running up the back of the man's neck. Mace K-9 had had his ear at the pub doors, just below the notices from the half-dozen city departments who'd had a hand in closing Willy's.

"Don't you keep some kinda record of who's got —"

"Sure we got records!" Mace K-9 said. "We got *lotsa* records! We got too *many* goddamn records which is how some get misfiled."

"I'd like to see those records," the constable said. Manny thought he was trying to look diligent for the benefit of the Board of Health.

"Well, we found 'em, now," Mace K-9 said lamely. "And what they say is whatcha got in there is ya got these two Dobies."

"Dobermans?" Manny asked.

Mace K-9 nodded.

"Hm," Manny said in a very unhappy way. "How long they been in there?"

"The place was seized last week," the Board of Health said.

Manny knew his eyes went wide because he could feel that goddamn wind cutting into them. "And nobody knew about them until *today?*"

"Hey!" the Board of Health said, holding up a hand, then pointing at the constable; "*They* closed the place!"

"Let's not get on that merry-go-round, again," Manny said.

"Then, today, a couple of kids tried breaking into the place —"

"Little pricks shoulda been in school where they belonged," Mace K-9 said.

"The dogs went after them —"

"Jesus!" Manny said.

"Hey, that's their *job!*" Mace K-9 said. "Shoulda been in school."

"Anybody else coming with you?" the constable asked.

"You mean..." and he nodded back at the car.

"I mean like Emergency Services. I thought they always sent those nuts in for stuff like this; *hut-hut-hut!*"

"That's what I thought, too," Manny said.

"We already tried getting in," the Board of Health said. "One of the dogs threw himself at the door. Violently."

"They get a little testy when they don't eat for a coupla days," Mace K-9 said dryly.

The ASPCA guy cleared his throat. "We should try to bring the animals in. Intact."

Manny turned to the Board of Health.

"Well, *I* don't *want* to have to shoot the dogs," the Board of Health said.

"Shoot the dog!" some of the crowd chanted. "Shoot the dog!"

"Christ," mumbled the constable.

Animal Control gave his nose another wipe with his glove. "I can't get a clear shot at 'em. A tranquilizer dart in his freakin' eye ain't gonna do much good."

Manny turned back to Mace K-9. "Aren't these dogs supposed to have some kinda code word —"

"Yeah, but he ain't listenin'. I tried the commands for *both* dogs since we don't know which one this is. No soap."

"I thought they were supposed to listen to those things."

"Yeah, they're *s'pose'* to. I think that dog has lost his shit is what I think. Look, he's in there almost a week with no food —"

"Maybe that's where the other dog went," the constable said.

"Ugh," Manny said.

"I think he's lost his shit," Mace K-9 said. "He ain't listenin' to nobody. I tell ya somethin'; that dog is *scared!* I *know* these dogs. I know what a scared dog is like! 'N' that is one, scared shitless dog!"

"So what do we do?" Manny asked, and then realized when those five faces turned to him that, evidently, coming up with an answer was considered his job. He held up a finger for them to wait and started back toward the squad. He could see Hanratty watching him, already shaking his head that this wasn't any of his fucking business, that he didn't want it to be any of his fucking business.

Manny slid into the car, almost sighed orgasmically in the snug heat.

"I don't wanna hear it," Hanratty mumbled.

"There's a problem."

"So, you're deaf 'sides bein' retarded."

Manny doped out the situation.

Hanratty flapped his lips signifying either he was thinking, exasperated, or just felt like flapping his lips. "It's cold out there, isn't it?"

"Yeah."

"I mean really fuckin' cold."

"It's pretty bad."

"Then fuck it. You go tell 'em, Paco —"

Manny twitched at "Paco."

" – it's their fuckin' problem."

"When we get back to the house, is that how you want me to write it up? We left because it was their fucking problem? You'll sign off on that, right?"

Hanratty flapped his lips, again, then reached for his cap. "You're a pain in my ass."

Manny shook his head wondering how this was in any way his fault then followed Hanratty out of the car and back to the front doors of Willy's.

"Here he comes!" said somebody from the crowd. "Here comes the big guy!"

Hanratty stopped, gave the crowd a quick glare, then turned to Manny. "Hey, Miguel, thems your people in there; whyntcha go tell 'em all to all go get a fuckin' job or somethin'."

Hanratty didn't introduce himself to the guys in Willy's doorway. He stared at the door for a second. "Fuck, it's cold." He stared for another second. "How 'bout this. What if we open this door, just a crack, ok? 'N' we fire a shot through just to scare Fido back a bit so Billy the Kid here —" meaning Animal Control " – can get a bead on him with his dart gun? How's that sound?"

"I don't like the guns," the ASPCA said.

"Ya like a dart in the eye better?" Animal Control said.

"I've got no problems with it," the Board of Health said. "Let's give it a shot. I mean, a try."

Hanratty nodded at Manny and nodded him toward the door. "G'ahead."

"Me?"

"Good guess."

"Shouldn't you do it? You're senior."

"That's discharging my service pistol in the line of duty. That's paperwork. If you think I'm doin' that kinda paperwork my last couple weeks, you can —"

"I get it."

Manny had never discharged his service pistol in the line of duty except on the pistol range and that was so long ago back in training he couldn't remember when that was. Other than that, Manny had never had his pistol out of its holster. It felt funny in his hand out there on the street.

"Stand back!" somebody in the crowd shouted. "Here comes the shit!"

Manny stood close by the seam of the two doors while the others cracked one open, keeping their collective weight on it to keep the dog inside. Even after a week without food, Manny thought the dog sounded pretty damn strong when he pounded into the door. The dog bit and clawed frantically at the wood, letting out a hysterical combination of barks and growls and yelps. Manny held his pistol above the pointed, black face trying to push through the gap and squeezed off a round.

The dog didn't back off.

"Shoot the dog!" the crowd chanted again. "Shoot the dog!"

"Maybe we should shoot one of *them*," Hanratty said. "Try it again."

The dog only flinched at the second shot even though Manny held his pistol closer. He tried a third shot. "Oops. I think I caught his ear."

The ASPCA guy had a shit fit over that, but it did persuade the dog to back off.

"Now!" Hanratty shouted.

They eased the door open a few inches more, the dart gun went *phhht,* and they slammed the door closed.

The crowd applauded.

"God, I hate these people," the constable said.

"You get him?" Manny asked Animal Control.

"I hope so."

"You got enough dope in that thing?" Hanratty asked.

"Christ, I hope so."

Animal Control checked his watch and when he said it'd probably be safe, they cracked the door open and waited. No dog. They let the door swing open.

The air inside the pub was stale and musty. It stunk of something rotting. They all craned their heads inside the door, following the sound of fast, shallow breathing. They saw the dog across the barroom behind some dusty tables. It was still standing although its legs were wobbly. The small, black marble eyes glinted in the gray light slicing through the ajar door.

"I thought you said he'd be knocked out," Hanratty said.

"He should be out on his ass," Animal Control said.

"Better give him another one."

"I don't want to o.d. 'im."

The Doberman growled. He didn't even sound drowsy.

"I'll get another dart," Animal Control said.

Mace K-9 hit the flashlight app on his cell phone and aimed the beam at the dog. "Jeeeeesus..."

The Dobie's body was loose flesh hanging on obvious ribs and jagged hips. His mean little eyes flashed despite the drug. The dart was still stuck in his bony hind quarters.

"He look rabid to you?"

"What the hell does rabid look like?"

"God, what stinks in here? Is that the other dog?"

"Ugh," Manny said.

"Sonofabitch should be on his ass," Animal Control said and let another dart go. The dog dropped almost immediately.

"Anybody see the other dog?"

Hanratty gave one of his just-barely nods at Manny. Manny pulled his flashlight from his utility belt, hit the switch and led them in. He considered drawing his pistol again, but that felt silly, him playing The Great Hunter for a couple of pooches. But he tightened his grip on his light because the old hairbags at the station always said that in a pinch, it made a good club.

The only one who didn't follow him into the bar was the constable. He stayed in the doorway chewing his mustache. "I've got a two-year degree in Law Enforcement," he said. "Not animal psychology."

They were fanning out across the barroom.

"Stroke!" Mace K-9 called out. "Stroke! Stroke!"

"That his name?" Manny asked.

"That's their code command to heel. I don't want that other one jumpin' outta the dark."

"Stroke!" Manny called out. "Strokestrokestroke!"

Manny and the others gathered around the tranquilized Dobie, except for Hanratty. Manny saw him heading for an archway to another room with tables, some kind of dining room he guessed. Animal Control nudged the dog with his boot to make sure the dog was out before the Board of Health shone his own cell phone light on the animal to examine him.

"He's all marked up," the Board of Health said. "Scratches, bites..."

"From the other dog?" Manny asked.

"These aren't dog bites. You keep those people out there clear!" the Board of Health shouted to the constable. He turned to Animal Control. "Take him out to the truck. Take him in. I want him tested for rabies right away."

"This one's Grizzly," Mace K-9 said, reading the dog's collar tag. "The other one's Attila."

"Nice names," the ASPCA said.

Mace K-9 started calling out to Attila.

Hanratty told him to shut up. "Listen! Hear that?"

They heard muffled *patpatpat* noises on the dusty floor in the other room, mixed with *ticktickticks;* little feet with little nails moving in the shadows along the walls.

"I want to find that other dog," the Board of Health said.

They all followed the strong reek into the other room. The smell was so strong there, Manny's eyes began to water.

"Jeee*esus*, it stinks in here!"

Manny thought he might be sick.

They followed the stink to a small alcove serving as a scullery.

"Holy shit..." the ASPCA man said.

There on the floor, in the criss-crossing beams of their lights, were bones, small bones. Rats. The dogs had put up a good fight for a while.

What was left of Attila was there, too. The rats had pretty well stripped the meat from the rear half of the dog. One brazen little bastard was still sitting there, facing them as he nibbled a sausage-type link from the Doberman's entrails.

"Let's get the fuck outta here!" somebody said, but Hanratty was already gone; Manny had never seen the big man move so fast, didn't think it was possible for him to motor like that.

The Board of Health ran straight to his car, got on his radio, started shouting about fumigation and maybe having the building condemned. When he was done, he posted a "Quarantine: Contagious Disease" sign on the closed doors because it was the only sign he had and the best thing he could think of to scare people away.

Manny and Hanratty sat in the squad for a few minutes. Hanratty was huffing, trying to catch his breath; Hanratty's sprint out of the bar was as much physical exertion as Manny had ever seen out of his senior since he'd been riding with him. For his part, Manny was trying to get his stomach to stop doing acrobatics. He'd close his eyes trying to will calm on his middle, but then he'd see poor Attila and that awful, gut-twisting smell would come back to him.

As soon as Hanratty had his breath back, he put the car in gear and headed them out.

"We should get back to the house," Hanratty said. "You got paperwork to do, Eagle Eye." Then he started to chuckle. "Just think, Chico, nineteen more years of this and you can retire!" The chuckle rumbled up into a hard, phlegmy laugh. Every time the *haw-haw-haws* would start to subside, Hanratty would mumble, "Just nineteen more years!" and the laughter would kick up again.

The fat fuck did that all the way back to the station house.

A SMALL PIECE OF HISTORY

(Authors Note: I'd only met him a few times, yet I thought of him as a friend, and I often flattered myself thinking he felt the same of me, though our bond had been formed by circumstance as much as anything else.

I'd literally bumped into him in a back hallway as MPs tried to sneak him into the Ft. Benning courtroom through a side door to avoid the media mob out front. We had a few minutes before going in and we began chatting. Meeting him after hearing even the little which had been released about the case, I was surprised at how young he was. From what had been said up to that point, I'd expected someone seasoned and hard. Instead, he was a pleasant-faced, affable fellow, and even at the time of his trial he smiled easily.

We didn't discuss the proceedings. We talked football — he hated baseball — and how he couldn't wait for the season to start. He told me how he'd tried out in high school but had been too short and too slow to qualify. "Story of my life," he said, "Too damn short, too damn slow." He asked me for gum, I gave him my last stick. Then, it was time to go inside.

It became a daily ritual after that, meeting in the dark, back hall, just me, him, and the MPs, and he had us all — even his escorts — chewing the fat comfortably, casually. Once seated in court, one could almost think of the young, blank-faced man sitting at the defendant's table as someone else; a stranger.

I'm not sure where the rapport came from. Maybe it was our closeness in age — I only had him by four years — or maybe because I'd been to Nam as well, stringing for one of the major weekly mags. Or maybe it was simpler; he needed a friend, someone he could talk to, and I was available.

I never pumped him about what had happened or used anything he said to me in that hallway in a piece. He didn't ask me not to, and I think he appreciated that he didn't have to. It was just understood. I imagine that's why he sent for me after the trial; he felt he could trust me.

Met out of uniform — he never wore the uniform well — with no knowledge of the trial, few would have disliked him. I know there are those who will balk at hearing that, and say they could smell the corruption in him, but that's arrogance, thinking we are beyond or above his actions; that he was some sort of "other." But there was nothing extraordinary about him, no alien-ness. He was one of us.

The interview took place a few months after the close of his trial in 1971. He did not want it released at the time fearing it would embarrass or cause discomfort to people he felt didn't deserve it, and, for that reason, though many years have passed since then, I have continued to accede to his wishes including that of omitting all names, and most identifying references and biographical details including his.

It's no great trick to figure out who he is. A trip to any local library can fill in that blank for any who care, and he surely must've known that. Still, this is how he wanted it, so that's how I've delivered it. He wanted this record to stand on its own, and that's how I've left it.

That in mind, you might ask why bother?

I would answer that it is not the names and places which are important; only the lesson.)

Q: There we go.

A: It's running?

Q: Yeah. See it?

A: Ok. So, how do we do this? I just talk?

Q: However, you want to do it.

A: Hm. I, uh… Boy, this is nothing like you think it's gonna be. I thought I had it all down in my head, ya know? Now — … Hmmm…

Q: Well, why don't you just start at the beginning.

A: Of what?

Q: You know. Home, how you got into –

A: All that log cabin crap? "It all began in a small cabin along the Whosis River —"

Q: *(laughing)* Well of course, you should only say what you want to say. I don't want this to be hard for you. Why don't we do this? Why don't you start by saying why you wanted to do this? For the record, people who hear this should know this was your idea.

A: Well, you said it: for the record. That's why. Ya know? 'Cause nowhere is it down, my side, that's not down anywhere. They told me to plea it out –

Q: You didn't have to.

A: You didn't have to be F. Lee Bailey to see where things were going. Let's face it, it was never a question of what I did. Plea it out, they said, and that'll finish it. Plea it out and you don't get hung.

Seemed like a damn good deal to me. And, ya know, I started figuring, after all, how hard were they gonna be on me? I don't want to sound, I dunno, what's a word, mercenary or anything, but it was my neck, right? So, I thought, look at — — and — —, look at what *they* did. One of 'em walks clean, and the other one gets a reduced sentence. And it's not like you see him out there bustin' rocks, right? And what *I* did wasn't near as bad as what — — did. I mean, look around. This isn't so bad. It's a regular apartment. Hell, I never lived in a place this nice. They tell me this is where they usually keep mob guys when they're waiting to testify for the feds. Look, I got a TV, stereo. It's not too bad. Kitchen, make my own food. Hey, you want something?

Q: No, I'm good, thanks.

A: There's even a pool table in the other room!

Q: You make it sound like they did you a favor.

A: Fuck, man, they did *themselves* a favor, don't let nothin' or nobody fool you 'bout that. Make me look bad enough to hang and they *all* look bad enough to hang. Plea it out, nobody testifies, it's over. This way, finish it, close the book. Sooner or later, everybody forgets.

Q: Then why bring it up again?

A: Like you said: for the record. I want it down somewhere, *somewhere,* I want it down, *my* side. It's not like I want it *out* there or anything, I'm not saying go put it on the front page of *The New York* fucking *Times,* I just want to know it's down somewhere. Does that make sense?

Q: I don't know. You're not denying you did it, am I right?

A: It's got nothing to do with who did what. I just want it —… I'm not looking for an out. It's just that *somewhere* it's down the way *I* saw it. Ok?

Q: It's your party. Look, it's up to you but I really do think we should go to the beginning, though. You want this for the record? People have a picture of you from all the press coverage. If you really want them to know the way you saw things, they have to know you.

A: I don't know how to do this.

(At this point, he turned off the recorder. He was adamant about not discussing his family or anything about his life at home. It was not shyness, nor was it self-consciousness.

Simply, he'd felt he'd given them enough pain and felt no need to, even inadvertently, risk giving them more.

But I will bend a rule here because, as I told him, - you should know him.

He was the youngest of four children – two brothers and a sister – born in 1946 to a working-class family in one of the dying factory towns of the northeast.

His mother worked in a bakery. As the youngest child, she doted on him.

His father, a factory worker, was a taciturn sort, uncomfortable with expressing his affection. But "He must've loved us," he told me, "'cause he worked like a dog to support us. And if there was some school thing, if you were gonna be up there singing "I'm a Little Teapot," and he wasn't working, he'd be there. But if you wanted a hug, you went to Mom.")

Q: What about school. Want to talk about school?

A: Do you? *(Laughs.)*

Q: Academics weren't your strong suit?

A: *Spider-Man* and *The Fantastic Four* was my idea of fine reading material.

Q: So you didn't even think about college.

A: I didn't have to. My mom and dad thought about it enough for all of us! They wanted us all to go although we never had the money for it. They thought it was like the Great American Success Pill. That's what you do: you go to school, then you go to college, and you live happily ever after working at something where you wear a suit and make wads of money. They didn't know. Look, they were like anybody else's parents, they wanted things to be good for us, and this was what they had in their heads would do it. What did they know? My sister, she married some kid from the neighborhood and that was it for her, but my brothers tried it, ya know, working their way through, but none of us had a head for school. Nobody did more than a year.

Q: So, college was out. That's when you joined the Army?

A: That makes it sound too simple.

Q: How complicated was it?

A: (Laughs.) Well, it got *real* simple after I saw how low my draft number was! But even if that wasn't the case…

Q: Yeah?

A: Look, no sense in dancing around it. I couldn't do a goddamn thing. I mean, like I had no fuckin' aptitude for *anything!* I'm out of high school looking at digging ditches, or maybe the old man can get me on at the factory where he was working. I saw how miserable it made him, so I thought, let me try a semester at (the nearest county college) but –

(blows a raspberry)

Q: Bad grades?

A: Like I said, none of us had much of a head for school. I was no exception.

Q: And still, the Army selected you for –

A: Wait, wait, you're getting ahead. You're the one who wanted to hear all this stuff.

Q: Sorry.

A: It's like you don't know what you *want* to do, but you sure as hell know what you *don't* want to do. So, I did the semester and there was this Army recruiter there on campus. It's not like he had to make a real sales pitch for me. There I am –

Q: You don't know what to do with yourself.

A: — right, and my draft number came up that year in low single digits, and with *my* grades, there was no fucking way I was getting a (college) exemption. Does that answer your question? Seriously, you see where I was?

Q: In a bad place.

A: Bad *fucking* place.

Q: What'd your parents think? How'd they react when you told them the news?

A: Well, mom, she's a mom, she was all broken up. The minute I said I put in my papers she already had me down for dead or maimed or something. Remember, this was, let's see, now this was '67, we'd already had the grunts in for two years by then, and every night on TV she sees it getting worse, so, of course, she's a mom, she's fucking terrified. She's *positive* her little baby is gonna get his ass shot off.

Q: Weren't you worried about that?

A: Funny, no. It just didn't seem — . I don't know if it was because I was young and cocky or young and stupid...or young and cocky and stupid...but before I went over I never worried about it. You don't think that kind of thing is real, you think it's always gonna be somebody else, *you're* gonna live forever.

Q: How about your father? How did he take the news?

A: Ya know, it was funny. My father wasn't a guy who showed much. That was the first thing – shit, the *only* thing I ever did — where he was out-there honest-to-God proud of me. You gotta remember, 'bout that time there were kids skipping off to Canada, burning their draft cards… And here I was, Mr. — —-'s little boy, taking up the sword – that's what he used to say, what he called it, "taking up the sword." He was a veteran, World War II, the Pacific, so this meant a lot to him. He really thought that was the coolest thing his son could do.

Q: After basic, you were accepted for OCS (Officer's Candidate School). I wouldn't think…

A: *(Laughs.)* You mean because I was such a fucking Einstein in school?

Q: Well…

A: Surprised me, too! I wasn't even thinking about it, but some OCS guy was looking for candidates, my platoon sergeant asked me 'bout it, he put me up…

Q: You were seriously thinking about the Army as a career by then? I mean, going for an officer's commission doesn't sound like you were just riding out your hitch.

A: I don't know how serious. Here's the thing. When it came to soldiering, and even the work you had to do in OCS, look, I still wasn't a guy for the books, I'm *still* not, but I had a knack for some things. I don't know why, and it wasn't like I was the OCS Man of the Year or anything, but I was pretty ok at it. So, I guess, starting out not knowing what I wanted to do with myself, then you find something you're good at…

Q: I get it. It's like you found your place.

A: I guess.

Q: I imagine your father –

A: Oh, man, when I came home with my second looie's bars? You would've thought I got the Congressional Medal of Honor or something. He took me around to all the bars where his buddies hung out, showing me off. And, I got to admit, I felt pretty good 'bout it, too.

Q: You found something you could do.

A: Yeah. I mean, it's not like I was thinking of becoming a twenty-year man or anything, but it felt good to accomplish something.

Q: So then…

A: So then nothing. One of the reasons I enlisted was they told us – this is the recruiter – that if you enlisted your chances of getting sent over to combat were just about zero. But I fucked myself with OCS. If I hadn't put in for it I probably woulda spent my whole hitch cleaning toilets or something. But now I'm an *officer*. A year went by, I made first lieutenant, and there was what you call a high attrition rate among lieutenants over there. So, wasn't too long I'm tagged to go over. I wound up a platoon commander with a detached company pulling "Palace Guard" duty at III Corp HQ in Saigon.

(Authors note: As the war wound on, the Army found its manpower situation squeezed on one side by the increasing scale of the U.S. commitment, and on the other, by its rotation policies.

Under the Kennedy Administration in the early 1960s, the American military commitment in Vietnam consisted of no more than several thousand advisors. By the time of the Tet

Offensive in 1968, the U.S. had over a half-million troops engaged in Vietnam. At the same time the Army needed more troops, it was going through them at an unprecedented rate.

In World War II, most men in service – no matter when they'd been inducted or enlisted – remained in uniform for the duration of the war. In Korea, the Army adopted a rotation policy based on a point system which could put a soldier on a ship home in as little as eighteen months. In Vietnam, the Army instituted a standard combat tour of 12 months [13 months for Marines]. However, believing combat experience was invaluable for officers, officers' tours were for only six months. As a result of the massively increased need for manpower and the constant rotation home of troops, by the end of the 1960s the Army was regularly dealing with shortages of quality personnel. The Army's response was to widen the pool of available manpower by loosening its standards.)

Q: This "Palace Guard" duty. What was that?

A: That, my friend, is dream duty. It's supposed to be an honor but that was horseshit. There was a *lot* of horseshit over there. You were there; you know.

Q: Yeah.

A: You know I had five guys in my platoon who'd never been out of Saigon who had Purple

Hearts? They'd bust a leg or sprain a wrist playing volleyball or some shit. They're at a bar, an RPG (rocket-propelled grenade) goes off down the block and one of the guys falls on his ass. The Army'd give him a fucking medal. It was supposed to be good for morale or something. It only depressed the shit out of me.

Q: What actually were your duties?

A: You stood around the doors and looked pretty on the weekly parade. I mean, technically, you were supplying security for the brass, but that was more horseshit. Grunts humpin' in the boonies would've given their eye teeth for that kind of assignment. What I heard was our company CO, Captain ——- , he was asshole buddies with one of the regimental commanders, and this regimental brass ass got us the assignment as a favor to his buddy.

Q: I see.

A: Now, the only reason (the company commander) was even *in* Nam is he wanted his CIB (Combat Infantryman's Badge) 'cause he figured that was the fastest way to his majority. You see why they didn't want a trial? All this horseshit – *unbelievable* horseshit – woulda come out.

Q: What about the other company officers?

A: Well, the company exec was this color guy from New Orleans. I'm sorry: *N'awlens*, that's how he taught me to say it. *(Laughs.)* He was good, a nice guy. Sharp, too. Lieutenant — —- . ROTC, really conscientious, ya know? Always sweatin' 'bout the men. The captain was always off ass-kissing with somebody, while Lieutenant — —- would take care of business. The rest of 'em, though — . They were ok, I guess. Some good, some not so good. We were not exactly America's fighting elite.

(Author's note: Another Army strategy to meet increasing manpower needs was to create new divisions. This particular "Palace Guard" company was part of one such unit.

These divisions, without the long-standing traditions of outfits with history [i.e. the 101st "Screaming Eagles" Airborne Division; the "Big Red One" First Infantry Division] had great difficulty establishing a sense of unit identity, cohesion, pride, and loyalty among their men. Worse, like expansion teams in professional baseball and football, their ranks were often filled with cast-offs from other units as well as new men coming in under the lower induction standards. During the trial, I once asked a senior officer who'd been a graduate of West Point about this particular situation. He told me that a year or so before the events described here, my young friend not only would never have graduated from OCS with a commission, he probably would never have been accepted into the program.)

A: Well, wait, there was this one guy, another platoon commander, he came into the outfit about the same time I did. Name was — —- . I think he'd gone to some military school. Not The Point. Some place down south. A real rah-rah. And he never listened to anybody. He was like in *The Wizard of Oz?* Ya know, you get a piece of paper and all of a sudden you're smart? Well, that was him, he got the paper, he thought he was smart.

Q: But he wasn't.

A: Well, maybe he was smart like he always knew which fork to use, and he could read without moving his lips. But, look, my platoon sergeant, — —- , this guy had twenty years in, ok? To me, he was the fucking voice of God. He said go that way, don't go this way, and I would. He'd had two tours as an advisor before I – thank God – got him. But this guy, he's been to fucking *school*, so he figured fuck all you guys! I'm a fucking military genius!

Q: How did you get along with your men?

A: Pretty good. I'm not bullshitting you. Really, I thought pretty good, and these were some rough dudes. I mean, I took my responsibility serious, ya know? The exec kept telling me, ya know, "That's your job, boy! They're looking to *you* to get their asses home!" I bought into that. I still do. And we got along because they knew I wasn't a dickhead. Look, I'm not saying I was fucking Eisenhower or anything, that these guys'd follow me into hell and all that crap, but they knew I wasn't some dickhead, I wasn't looking to do something stupid, or showboat. Now, the guys, they looked over at this ——- bozo, they're thinking, "Dickhead!" Like, every time you signed out a jeep or truck, when you brought it back, he made you clean it, grease it up, change the oil. *Every* time. You made a ten minute run to get the mail, when you got back, wipe it down, get out the grease gun, change the oil. And every day, he'd get up a detail of off-duty guys, take 'em out on a four-by, go out into the bush a click or two and make 'em dig.

Q: Dig what?

A: A hole! What else do you dig? He'd have 'em just dig this big hole, put the dirt on the truck, go down the road another click and shovel it out. Next day, he'd come back out there with *another* detail, they shovel the pile of dirt back into the truck, go back and fill in the hole. This went on and on and finally, one day, the guys just fucking had it! They throw down their shovels and say, Fuck you! He was gonna have 'em all busted but the exec talked him out of it. What're you gonna charge 'em with? "They refused to obey my stupid, pointless order to keep doing this stupid, pointless thing!" What the fuck is that? You're gonna bust 'em they didn't want to dig a fucking hole?

Q: And you were different from someone like him.

A: (*Laughs.*) *Everybody* was different from him! The rest of us, we're, "We've got it easy! Why fuck with it?" You had spare time – and you pull that kind of duty, you have a *lot* of spare time – you gonna spend it digging holes?

Q: How'd you spend *your* spare time?

A: The way everybody does. You drink. You go to the bang-bang shops on Tu Do Street. Sometimes you had to do something crazy to keep from *going* crazy because most of the time it was just so goddamn boring. Like this one night, I took some of my guys, we walked down to this electronic surveillance outfit, we went up to the guards and I said, "We're here about the trailer." They just waved us through, they didn't give a shit, we weren't gooks so we must be ok. We hook this half-million dollar surveillance trailer to a four-by, drive off with it and left it on the lawn at the officer's mess. (*Laughs.*)

Q: Were all the officers like you? New to the outfit?

A: Well, actually, the company'd been on post for a couple months before I got there. I was a replacement. Listen to this. This is good! The CO was trying to make points with his buddy up at regiment, right? Now somehow – don't ask me why – getting the grunts in the field to buy money orders is supposed to be a way of doing it. The grunts buy the money orders and send them home to their families. It's supposed to make the outfit look good all these kids sending money home. So, the CO grabs (his predecessor), packs him in a slick with a footlocker full of money orders and sends him out into Indian Country. This looie's never been out of Saigon since he got there and they dumped him on some rifle company with this footlocker full of money orders! Boom! There was a mortar barrage and this guy's chopper cut ass out without him. The way I heard it, they had just come down for a touch-and-go, he was standing on the skid, boom, the first shell went off, and they just fucking pushed this poor bastard out, the chopper guys, and throw him his footlocker full of money orders, and they split. He was out there in the middle of the LZ, hugging his money orders with the shit coming in and the grunts were in their holes laughing their asses off. But, ya know, it didn't work out too bad for him. This guy wound up taking some shrapnel in his ass – I mean that, literally, the stupid sonofabitch didn't know enough to keep his ass down — and the prize for being that stupid is a ticket home.

Q: You're in Saigon, very cushy duty it sounds like. How did you go from that to being in-country?

A: Well, it was that dickhead (company commander) and his CIB. Apparently, no matter how many friends you have upstairs pushing for you, you can't twist sitting on your ass in Saigon playing golf – these guys had their own golf course, you believe that? Anyway, no matter how you bullshit it, you can't turn that into the thirty days in the field you need to qualify for your CIB. So, this dickhead, he saw his tour was winding down, he went to his buddy at regiment and put us in for a transfer to a firebase.

Q: I'll bet that went over real well with the men.

A: Like a case of the crabs. And the CO, what does he give a shit? It's not like *he* was gonna be doing any serious humpin'. *He* was gonna be sitting in his hooch playing canasta or some shit –

Q: He didn't go out?

A: Every so often. Easy patrols.

Q: Was he, um…

A: You trying to be diplomatic?

Q: *(Laughs.)* I guess.

A: Much as I didn't think there was a bigger dick in the outfit, I don't think he was yellow. I just think he didn't want to work up a sweat, ya know? Look, there were good officers and bad officers everywhere you went, ok? Some guys were fire-eaters, some of 'em were hard as nails, they shit A(rmor) P(iercing) rounds. Like the exec; he was a really decent guy. But the CO, thirty days sittin' on his ass in his hooch was enough to get him his CIB and that's all he gave a shit about.

(Author's note: The firebase was in Hua Nghia province two day's march from the Cambodian border near the tip of what was called "The Fishhook," a curved section of Cambodia arcing into Vietnam. It was the closest point between Viet Cong sanctuaries in Cambodia and their most prized targets: Saigon and the major military installations surrounding the city such as the airfield at Bien Hoa. Military Intelligence speculated the province was home to several "off ramps" of the two main routes the Viet Cong and North Vietnamese used to move supplies and troops south. The maze of trails collectively known as "The Ho Chi Minh trail" wound down from North

Vietnam through Laos and Cambodia. Munitions and personnel were also landed by sea on the Cambodian coast and moved up along the so-called "Sihanouk Trail." After a quarter-century of nearly unbroken combat with the Japanese, French, the South Vietnamese government, and the Americans, the Cong – some of whose leaders had been serving in the field all that time – knew each path, hill and stream, and had set up elaborate underground tunnel systems in the area. The firebase, on the other hand, had only been fully operational since June of 1967.)

A: It killed me; we ship out to Firebase — —- , and Captain Dickhead doesn't make the trip.

Q: Where was he?

A: Still in Saigon! Had a case of the running shits. So they said. I just think he didn't want to leave his air conditioning.

Q: How was life at the firebase?

A: It was a fucking hole. Hot and dusty. A slick would come in, kick up the dust and it'd take forever to settle. Fucking dust in everything. The food, your water, you were always breaking out in a rash because it got in your clothes everywhere and rubbed you raw. You were constantly cleaning your weapon. A 16 (M-16 assault rifle) is so fucking fragile you get an ant's eyelash in there and it jams. Then, when the fucking monsoons came, all that dust turned to mud. Right up to the hip. No, I mean it; to your fucking *hip!*

Q: Was there much action out there?

A: Well, going out we'd heard it was a pretty hot sector, but, all in all, it turned out kind of boring. Every once in a while the VC would lob some mortar shells in, just to shake your ass up, but other than that… One guy built seventeen model airplanes in the time I was there, mounted them on cut-up 105 (105 mm howitzer) casings just to pass the time.

Q: What's the matter? You're making a face?

A: Well, it *was* quiet, there at the firebase. But that Lieutenant — — ? The one with all the digging the holes? That's where they fragged him.

Q: Who fragged him?

A: Could've been anybody. Tell you the truth, I was surprised it hadn't happened back in Saigon. Look, we're in-country, you know the Indians are out there even if it's quiet. Nobody was looking for trouble, but this dickhead was always volunteering his people to go out in the bush, ambush patrols and stuff. His people were getting pissed with him. I guess he took them out one time too many. One night, somebody rolled a frag under the flooring in his hooch. Ya know, I didn't like him either, but still...

Q: I guess you're always thinking, once they do that, they might do it to anybody.

A: I guess.

Q: So now you're at the firebase.

A: Yeah. I guess we were there, maybe a coupla three weeks before — ... Hey, you want a smoke?

Q: Thanks.

(Sound of cigarettes being lighted. He coughs.)

Q: Maybe you should cut back.

A: I'm gonna have to; I'm almost out. The MPs pick them up for me at the PX, but I forgot to ask. Maybe I'm just going through them faster.

Q: You were saying...

A: Oh, yeah. Ya know, sometimes we actually thought it was safer being in-country then being in Saigon. There were always all these refugees coming into the city from the boonies and a lot of Cong were coming into town with them. You'd go to some bang-bang shop, you're doing your thing, and boom! You get an RPG up your ass. At least out in the field, you knew they were out *there* and you were *here*. You didn't have to watch your back as much that way.

Q: In the field.

A: That's a bitch, huh? Except when you were dealing with the fuckin' ARVNs (Army of the Republic of Vietnam – the South Vietnamese army).

Q: I heard a lot of stories.

A: You must've seen some shit, too.

Q: Some.

A: Then you know what I'm saying. I mean, hey, I saw a few good ARVN grunts but fuck…

(Author's note: Problems with the ARVN's performance were constant and endemic. Each time there was a change in the Saigon government – and, over the course of the U.S. involvement, coups happened regularly – the ARVN would be purged of officers considered loyal to the previous regime and stocked with officers loyal to the new one, loyalty being more prized than competence. It was a situation ripe for incompetence, corruption, and infiltration, all of which did

*little to inspire cohesion and esprit among the rank-and-file
ARVN troops, or much confidence by their U.S. allies.)*

A: We had an ARVN rifle company with us at the firebase. There was this lieutenant, I don't know what the fuck his name was, one of those gook Muck Wuck Fuck names, and we all knew that sonofabitch was in the black market. He was carrying forty-odd men on his platoon roster and I don't think he had two dozen live guys under him. They'd pay somebody to enlist, he went on the roster, they gave 'em a few bucks to split, but they kept him on the roster and kept his pay when it came in. Look, even if you were a good guy in the ARVN, you wanted to do your patriotic duty or some shit, you gonna fight for a fuck like that? And when we did mix it up with the Charlies, you know how many times we're doing the body count and find 'em carrying U.S. gear –

*(End of tape. New tape begins. Sounds of him rising from
his seat, pacing.)*

A: Hm.

Q: Are you ok?

A: This is harder than I thought.

Q: We can stop.

A: Yeah.

(Pause of eighteen seconds. Sound of a cigarette being lit, sound of him taking his seat again.)

A: You see 'em out there? I can see the parade ground from here. Sometimes I sit here and I can just watch for — . Look at this. See that one little bitty guy there in the last rank? Can't quite get it in gear. C'mon, boy! Shake your ass! Now look! The sarge is gonna give him some serious shit.

Q: Do you miss it?

A: What? Oh. You a good writer?

Q: Pretty good.

A: You like what you do?

Q: I do.

A: You miss it if you couldn't do it anymore?

Q: I see.

(Pause of six seconds. Sound of a deep sigh.)

A: Ok, ok.

Q: Are you all right?

A: The CO at this firebase, he was ok, he was one of the good ones. He figured let's all just do our tours and get the hell home with our asses in one piece. But then we got this new guy. Saigon never liked a zone when it was quiet. They wanted body counts. When things were quiet, no body counts. You can't be winning the war if you're not running up the count. So they sent this real GI type in. He wasn't a dickhead or anything, a very savvy guy, but he'd never been in-country before. It always took a while for these guys to understand how it worked. Ya know, they put out these missions, sweeps, trying to catch Charles. Charles wouldn't fight. Send out a column, he waited for it to go by. Charles just went around what he didn't want to deal with. Cherries came out, they didn't understand that. Send out a company, Charles disappeared. Send out a platoon, Charles came out in company strength; that's how he liked to fight. These brass asses back in Saigon would go on and on about what a chickenshit Charles was. He doesn't fight fair, boo-hoo! Well, *yeah!* So they were always coming up with these fucking brainstorms to draw Charles out, like Charles was as new to this as they were. The exec, a real book guy I told you, he read up on all this stuff. They been fighting here hundreds of years, he said, fighting the Chinese, the Cambodes… You really think some brass ass with a couple years of West Point and a few years post duty back home is going to fake Charles out?

Q: And this new firebase commander, he had one of these brainstorms?

A: He put us out on a search and destroy. Three days we were supposed to be in the bush. The slicks were gonna drop the whole company next to where G-2 heard there was supposed to be this big weapons and rations cache. We were supposed to have ARVN platoons on each flank which scared me more than the fucking gooks. We sweep through to this place, Quan My, and push toward the river (an upper branch of the Mekong) away from the Cambode border. The idea was any Cong in front of us get penned against the river. There was supposed to be another American company on the other side of the river; they were the anvil. Hammer into anvil, squash, then we board boats and come home.

Q: Who was in command at this time? Was Captain — —- still back in Saigon?

A: Yeah, still, so the exec, Lieutenant — —- , the guy I told you about, he was in command. And everything started out ok. We slicked in, our advance units practically fell into a Cong tunnel complex. We had a couple guys, little dudes, they were our designated "tunnel rats." But they don't want to go in. Well, one guy did go in, he started screaming and they pulled him out. You ever see tunnel rats at work?

Q: Once. Couple of years later at Cu Chi.

A: So you know what I'm talking about. You tied a rope to him in case he got zapped so you could pull him out. He was screaming so they pulled him out, but what he was yelling about are all these fucking spiders! *(Laughs.)* He wasn't worried 'bout booby traps or bumping into Charlies or anything. The place was full of bugs and *that's* why he won't go in. So, we just poured gasoline down the tunnel, lit it off with a willie peter (white phosphorous grenade), then scouted the brush for smoke coming out of any other holes. We found some other holes, poured more gas and grenades down *those* holes and sealed 'em up with satchel charges. We came out of this, we were feeling pretty good. No Cong, Charles probably lit out, but we busted up some of his tunnels, we were doing ok. We got maybe half a click past the tunnel, and we were out in a field of high elephant grass and boom! Mines. Bouncing Betties (so-called because they spring into the air after they're triggered, detonating about waist-high; packed with ball bearings, they're designed not so much to kill as to demoralize by wounding and maiming troops). Now we're stuck in this fucking minefield and, because things can always get worse, we start taking sniper fire. The ARVN flanker platoons miss the field. I don't know if those pricks knew the field was mined or not, but they were north of where they were supposed to be. The exec tried to get the ARVNs on the RT (radio telephone) to clear out the snipers, but the cocksuckers never answered. We were taking fire out in that goddamn grass for an hour before we got a flight of Hueys and Cobras (helicopter gunships) in to clear the snipers. Man, that was a *looong* fucking hour! You just stayed down hugging the dirt. Put your head up above the grass and Luke the Gook took it right off. It was too much for the exec. That's when he started to flake.

Q: You're talking about a mental collapse?

A: His boys were getting picked off, he snapped. You'd be down in the grass, you hear the Cong snipers, then somebody'd be screaming, "Medic!" And that was going on for an hour. The exec got up, started running around yelling about his men. One of the snipers knocked him down which was a good thing. Knocked him down before he could trip a mine. He got medevaced out with the wounded.

Q: That's when you assumed command.

A: The exec's on his way to the hospital, the CO's still back in Saigon with the shits, they hadn't replaced that military school dickhead yet, the one who got fragged, the Weapons Platoon is back at the firebase. That left me and the other rifle platoon lieutenant. He was actually senior to me, by a little bit, but he didn't want it. He said to me, "You take it. I can't hack this."

Q: So now you're in command of the company, the three rifle platoons. And how long had you been in Vietnam up to that time?

A: Four months, but we'd only been out in the field, at this firebase, a couple weeks.

Q: That's a hell of a lot of responsibility for a platoon lieutenant with just a few weeks action under his belt.

A: I'm not arguing with you, but what was I supposed to do? That's what they give you the bars for. There was nobody for *me* to dump it on like (the other platoon commander) did. And it's not like I didn't break a sweat over it. It took a few seconds for it to sink in, but when it did I just wanted to *shit*. I'm thinking, oh *man*...

Q: Ok, you're in command. You get out of the mine field. Then what?

A: We bivouac on this hill for the night. The night was quiet, thank God. I'm thinking maybe what happened back in the minefield was as bad as it was going to get and we were over the hump. Next day, we moved into Quan My. It's just this little hamlet. You know; a bunch of hooches, paddies. You've seen these little Dogpatch villes.

Q: Yeah.

A: Only the Cong's already been there. They probably came through soon's we dropped a Daisy Cutter to cut out the LZ ("Daisy Cutters" were massive 1000 lb. bombs dropped to flatten a section of jungle to quickly create helicopter Landing Zones). Quan My was the only place on the map within marching distance, so they had to figure sooner or later that's where we were going to end up. They'd come through that morning to remind the civilians who was really the boss. There'd been a short squad of Puffs in the hamlet, but when the Cong showed up they disappeared ("Puffs" were paramilitary self-defense forces drawn from the local populace). Couldn't blame 'em; they were never a match for hardcore VC cadre. Hoping Puffs would fight was like giving your grandpa an old M-1 and telling him the Red Army just landed outside of town; "Go get 'em!" Yeah, right.

(Pause of thirty seconds. Several times there's a sound like someone starting to speak.)

I'm getting hoarse all this yakking. That's one thing I miss.

Q: What?

A: A drink. I'm not allowed in here. Booze. Or broads. Once in a while, one of the MPs – I don't want to say which, I don't want to get him in trouble – once in a while he sneaks me a pint. It's not like I go on a bender or anything, just a shot once in a while. Sometimes it helps me sleep. I could use one right now.

(Short pause.)

Wow, I thought this was all cold, ya know?

Q: My father was in World War II. He had nightmares up through the 1950s.

A: I believe it.

(Pause for ten seconds, then the sounds of the lighting of a cigarette.)

I don't know what I'm gonna do when these are gone.

Q: We can stop.

(Sound of a sigh.)

A: We go into the ville. The Charlies had dragged the chief and his family out, cut 'em up really bad. Wife, kids…three kids, I'm talking about five, six years old, something like that. They strung the wife up first. She was pregnant. I don't know how far along. Pretty far. They opened her up like a fish. They beat the kids. With their weapons. Whipped 'em with barbed wire…

(Short pause, then the sound of a sigh.)

Then they strung up the chief, castrated him, then disemboweled him. He must've been happy as hell when they finally slit his throat.

(Sound of someone crossing the room, sound of water running in a distant sink, he returns to his chair. A cigarette is lit.)

> Q: You already have one going.
>
> A: Yeah?
>
> Q: Right there.
>
> A: Shit.
>
> Q: You all right?
>
> A: I just hate the idea of wasting these, I'm almost out.

(Short pause.)

So… There we are. And the other gooks, the civilians, they're just lookin' at us. We're asking, "Which way did they go?" And they look at you like they're going, "You asking *me?*" So, fuck 'em. The gooks.

> Q: Well, eventually you'd leave and they'd still be left with the Cong.
>
> A: Fuck 'em anyway.

Q: What did you think of the South Vietnamese? I don't mean the ARVNS. Generally.

A: I didn't.

Q: I mean –

A: I didn't really have much to do with 'em. When we were in Saigon, who did I see? We went to the bars on Tu Do Street or the pussy palaces at Penang. There were old mama-sans'd come out to clean up. When we were out in the bush, what? I saw them sometimes out in the paddies, on the river, they gave you this big dumbfuck smile, waving, like you're asshole buddies, but the vets were there telling you, "Hey, any one of 'em could be Charles." Young, old, man, woman, grown-up, kid, any one of 'em. I knew guys who really gave them shit. I just kept my distance. Better safe than sorry.

Q: Except in Penang.

A: (*Laughing.*) Well, *yeah!*

Q: You're in the hamlet.

A: We searched the place. No weapons, no Cong supplies, another piece of G-2 masterwork, right? We found this large store of rice. Maybe it was Charles's, maybe the gooks' in the village, didn't matter. SOP (standard operating procedure) was you burned any large cache of rice so we burned it. As we were sweeping through the ville, we found another one of the chief's family, a daughter, maybe sixteen. She was pregnant, too, and she was in labor. I mean she was ready to *pop!* Seems her hubby hid her when the Cong came, then he ran off into the bush. It was getting dark by this time so I had us dig in. The next day, we'd walk the few clicks to the river, meet the pick-up boats and we'd be done. That was the plan. In the meantime, we helped 'em clean up the place, a couple of the medics volunteered to help the girl with the baby. Ok, fine, all very good-guy Americans. We set up a perimeter, everything was quiet. Again, I was thinking maybe the worst was behind us, we just have the walk tomorrow and we're home. Then, around 0200, we started getting incoming. Two, maybe three (mortar) tubes, light at first, harassing fire. We dug in, we waited for 'em and sure as shit they hit us just before dawn. This wasn't cadre either; these were NVA regulars. They almost punched through because the fucking ARVNs were useless. Their whole side of the perimeter started to fold, at least this one platoon. The other ARVN platoon, I gotta say, the little rooster who ran it was something. He got his job like the rest of 'em – he was somebody's uncle or cousin or some shit – and he had his hand in the till like the rest of 'em, but the little sonofabitch was fucking fearless. I gotta say, if it wasn't for him I'm not sure we could've held. So, we had the NVA trying to breach the perimeter and they were fighting like goddamn alley cats, but we'd set out our booby traps and I was on the RT calling in our own heavy stuff –

Q: Artillery.

A:— yeah, I got it coming in and the gooks were taking a pounding. This goes on for a couple hours, then they pulled back into the bush. Great. We got the boss his body count, we kicked the shit out of 'em, let's get the fuck home.

(Author's note: The date of the NVA attack on Quan My was January 30, 1968 – the first day of the infamous Tet Offensive. To decisively prove American attempts to pacify the country had failed, Viet Cong cadre, along with supporting NVA units, attacked targets throughout South Vietnam. Later assessments of the action at Quan My theorized the NVA unit

in action there had probably been en route to attack a more substantial target, possibly the nearby firebase, but had taken advantage of the opportunity to fall on the American/ARVN units isolated in the hamlet. In all probability, had the company's search and destroy mission been mounted a few days earlier, or after Tet, the company – at worst – would have been subject to some light hit-and-run enemy action or, more likely, no action at all which would have been typical of ground operations in the area.)

A: I passed the word to everybody to displace and we were going to shag ass for the river. Then the medics came up to me and said they couldn't leave this pregnant girl. It's a breach, they said, the birth. Ya know, where the baby's all turned around. They said without their help maybe she wouldn't make it, maybe the baby wouldn't make it, we couldn't leave her. For sure, we leave and the gooks come in…she's had it. Then we got hit again.

Q: The North Vietnamese?

A: They were back and they were *pissed*. They *wanted* us! I never saw this before. This wasn't just to shake up the round-eyes! These guys wanted our fucking scalps! I got the medics screaming at me we couldn't leave this gook chick, I got my people screaming at me the whole fucking perimeter is collapsing. I didn't know how many gooks we were fighting –

Q: The after-action reports estimated two NVA companies, possibly a battalion.

A: And this wasn't little Luke the Gook in his little pajamas! These were NVA regulars! Hardcore. I told my people, "Form up, we're gonna have to fight our way out, maybe fight all the way to the river!" I called for artillery and air support and that's when I found out the firebase had their own problems, they were hot (under fire), they didn't have anything to spare. I went into the hooch where the medics were with this girl and I told 'em, "That's it! Let's go!" They started up again about the girl and I said, "Either take her or leave her but we're out of time!" And then…

(Pause of ten seconds.)

Q: That's when it happened.

A: This… Man… This is hard…

Q: Do you want to stop? It's ok if you do.

A: We're there. Let's just, you know…

Q: Take your time.

(Pause of twenty-one seconds. Sounds of someone pacing, then stopping a distance away.)

A: I don't know what that sergeant told that little guy, but look at him. He's on the beat now. Atta boy, hup, hoop, hareep, *hore…*

Q: Here's what the medics said at the preliminary hearing. Is it ok if I read this?

(Pause of seven seconds. Unintelligible noise.)

The medics said they told you the girl would die without their help. They said you pushed them aside and fired your weapon at the girl, then pushed them outside and joined your company fighting its way out of the hamlet. Is that what happened?

(Pause of ten seconds.)

A: I know I fired… I don't remember actually pulling the trigger, but I know… Then my 16 was empty.

(Author's note: There's a break in the recording here. I'd switched off the machine. He was in pretty bad shape. He went into the bathroom for a few long minutes. The recording begins again:)

A: Want to hear something make your head spin? They were going to decorate me. No, really! You probably won't get anybody to admit it now, but, no bullshit, they were going to put me up. Not because of Quan My, but we fought our way to the river, the NVA never broke contact with us. Just constant shit. The company that was supposed to be across the river, the anvil, they'd been landed on the wrong side. They thought we were Charles coming up behind them. We wound up shooting at each other for Christ knows how long before I got them on the RT, and even then I had to run out between us, let 'em see me to get them to cease fire. Then we had to hold the riverbank for two hours until the landing craft and PBRs (Patrol Boat River – small, armed boats) could extract us, and all the time the gooks are hitting us. When we debriefed later, (the firebase commander), he's going nuts, he thinks we're fucking John Wayne. "Hell of a stand!" he said, really kicked the shit out of the enemy. I think he missed the part about two of his companies kicking the shit out of each other, but, anyway, he said he was going to put me up and get a citation for the whole company. Course that didn't happen.

(Author's note: Of the 121 men in the company's three rifle platoons who went into the search and destroy operation, 16 were killed, 27 wounded. The losses suffered by the ARVN units were much higher. The Army after-action report of the three-day operation states that "nearly 100 of the enemy were killed" although there was never an opportunity to make an actual body count.)

A: Here's something else to make you laugh. Nobody acted like I did anything wrong! Not *then*. Nobody was happy about it, but everybody let it go. It was just more of the shit that happened. There was so much shit always going on out there… I'm not even sure how the story broke.

Q: Some reporters in Saigon heard the story. It was floating down the grapevine. Then a photographer from — —- got wind of it, he decided to run it down and see if there was anything to it.

A: So, if it hadn't been for that…

Q: You think it would've stayed quiet? You don't think any of the men would've said anything?

A: I dunno. Maybe. People forget.

Q: You think they would've forgotten something like that?

A: Man, people forget what they *want* to forget! And *that's* something they'd all *want* to forget.

Q: *You* haven't forgotten.

A: No.

Q: Think you ever will?

A: I hope so. Man, nobody wants shit like that in their head forever.

Q: When the news broke, how did your family take it?

(At that point, he reached over and turned off the machine. "That's it," he said, and that's how we ended it.

I saw him one more time. His sentence had been cut short and he was released in 1976, a year after Saigon fell. There was a rumor of ill health although it was never substantiated. The records do show that some of the areas where his company had operated near Cambodia had been sprayed with defoliant agents, including Agent Orange, as part of the long-running defoliant program Operation Ranch Hand.

There weren't many reporters present at his release. He seemed to have known I'd come, even though I hadn't sent him any notification, because he had an MP search me out of the crowd. The MP took me to the outbuilding where he was being held in pre-release. They were going to send him out a side gate to avoid what few press people had shown up. "Just like the old days, right?" he said when he saw me.

He still had the same, easy smile, but he didn't look well: pale and tired. It could simply have been a product of the four years of confinement and too many cigarettes, but I recalled the rumors about his health.

On my way to his release, I'd thought about what I should ask him if the opportunity arose: his thoughts on the outcome of the war, the years of social unrest which had passed while he'd been confined, and the other front-page touchstones of the time.

But I didn't.

We simply took up our chatting as if those moments in the corridor outside the courtroom were just yesterday. We mourned the loss of miniskirts, the perennial losing streak of his favorite football team, and so on. Then, it was time to go. He shook my hand, said, "See you around," and was gone.

The rumors of illness must have been true because a year later I heard he was dead, found in a hotel room in some small town in Montana he'd been passing through, identified by the contents of his wallet. His family wouldn't claim the body, and his court martial had removed any obligation the military had, so he was buried in Montana, far from his native ground, at municipal expense.

I saw a copy of the death certificate. The cause of death was listed simply as, "Undetermined." There'd been no autopsy.

Nobody had wanted the story; not then, not now. At first, it was still too recent, the war still too fresh and painful in people's minds, the subject still too sensitive. I was told people were eager to put the war behind them; they weren't ready to deal with it. Then came the belated "Welcome Home" euphoria and I was told the fences had been mended and there was no reason to dwell on the more unpleasant aspects of the war. And after, when the "Welcome Home" banners had come down, the war became ancient history, as removed and irrelevant – and uninteresting – as Korea, or the Spanish/American War. No one cared.

He was right about that, I suppose. I had thought as long as people could dream they could have nightmares, and if they could have nightmares they couldn't forget what had happened at Quan My. But they did.

Why bring it up now? Why bring it up at all?

There have been a few wars since he and I sat over the tape machine that day, and maybe some people should look at this before they fight the next few. And, it's worth having this out there for no other reason than the one he gave: for the record, so that somewhere it's down, reminding us it has happened before and it will happen again, and the lesson is there if only we take the time to study it.)

FURLOUGH, NOVEMBER 1944

At the sight of his uniform, the woman's eyes had gone wide and she began to waver on her legs. For a moment, Reitz thought she might collapse against the door, closing it in his face. He reached out with his good hand and took her under the elbow.

"It's all right, Mrs. DiFeo. Nothing's wrong."

She didn't hear. Or didn't believe. He slipped through the partly open door, supporting her as best he could.

"Mom? What's the matter, Mom? Is she all right?"

Quick glance into the other room; two girls – (what had Tommy told him? Twelve and fourteen?) – in their Sunday best, coats on, broad-brimmed hats of white straw, two sets of dark eyes turned sharply on him. The older one: afraid. For her mother. Of this stranger. That would be Sylvia. Little Sylvie.

But the younger one. No fear. The little cupie doll face strangely hard, angry. "What did you do to my mom?" That would be Concetta. Connie. Coco, Tommy called her.

"Would you get your mom a glass of water, please?" Reitz asked. Connie went to the sink, not taking suspicious eyes off him.

The entry door opened onto a cramped, eat-in kitchen. He lowered the woman into a chair and smiled as disarmingly as he could. "Mrs. DiFeo – Eve — everything is fine. Your husband – Tommy — he just wanted me to come by. He wanted me to bring you a letter."

"A letter?"

"Nothing bad. No bad news, I promise. Tommy thought since I had to pass through, I could carry a letter home for him. That's all."

"He's all right?"

"He complains about his back, his stomach, his feet, but yes, Tommy's perfectly fine."

Finally, a weak smile from her.

"Look…" He fumbled his one good hand inside his coat and uniform jacket and came out with an envelope.

The sense of relief overwhelmed her. Tears began to well up. She turned away, wiping at her eyes with her white-gloved hands. "I'm so sorry. This is embarrassing."

"No, it's not," Reitz soothed.

Then, suddenly, turning back with concern for him. "Are you all right?" She pointed to his left arm in its sling in a white cast.

"It only hurts when I salute." He burlesqued bringing up the encased arm and crashing it into his forehead.

She chuckled.

"I thought a salute was with the right arm," Connie said coolly.

The woman gave a quick, reproving glare to her daughter. "Girls, this is a friend of Daddy's. You are a friend of Tommy's, aren't you?"

Reitz nodded. "Alvin Reitz, Mrs. DiFeo. Tommy and I shared a room in Rome." He thought of a better recommendation and pulled back the sling so she could read the writing awkwardly scrawled across the face of the cast:

I'LL BET YOU DID IT ON PURPOSE!

XOX TOMMY XOX

She laughed, more than she should have, but it was as much in catharsis as amusement. She stood. "Do you mind? I have to put myself back together."

"I should go —"

"No, please."

"You look like you were getting ready to go out."

"We were going to mass."

"Mass?"

"Yes."

"Church," Connie said as if speaking to a child.

Reitz shook his head.

"What's the matter?" the woman asked.

"I've been traveling for something like three weeks. I didn't know what day it was; that this was a Sunday. I really should leave —"

"Please," she said and waved at him to stay in his chair. "I'll just be a minute. There's coffee on the stove. It's still hot. Girls, show Mr. —"

"Lieutenant," Connie said, noting the gold bars on his shoulder straps. "That's right, isn't it? Lieutenant?" But she knew.

"Yes," Reitz said. "Lieutenant Reitz. Alvin."

The woman retreated behind a curtain to a bedroom. He could hear her sniffle, then the clatter of cosmetic jars. The noise made him smile. It reminded him of his own wife.

Little Sylvie set a cup and saucer down in front of him, along with a sharply ironed linen napkin. She toted the pot over from the stove and poured. "Would you like milk? Sugar? We don't have much sugar —"

"This is fine, black is fine. You're Little Sylvie. That's what your dad calls you."

"He told you about me?" She tilted her head coyly, already the practiced coquette at fourteen.

"He told me about all of you. He misses you a lot."

"What'd he say about me?" This from a leery Connie.

"What did he tell me about Coco?"

She flushed at his use of the name.

"I think the word he used most often was, 'buster.' 'Little Sylvie is a sweetie,' he'd say, 'but Coco – she's a buster!'"

For the first time, Connie softened a bit, proud of her reputation.

"And even though you're a buster, he still misses you."

She turned away, not wanting him to see her face. Behind him, a doorway led to the parlor. He stood, and as he passed Connie, he patted her gently on the shoulder. She surprised him by not flinching away.

The shotgun apartment had four, small, square rooms, but the woman had made a liar of the drab face the tenement had presented to the street. She kept the rooms bright, clean, and comfortable. There was some odd-looking creature of papier mache sitting atop the cathedral radio, something obviously made by one of the kids. Reitz had to look closely to tell it was supposed to be a turkey.

"Which one of you made this?"

Little Sylvie, playing at modesty rather transparently, raised her hand.

"It's very good!" Reitz said.

Connie rolled her eyes. "I couldn't even tell it was a bird when she brought it home."

"I couldn't tell you were human when mom and dad brought you home!" was Little Sylvie's retort.

Connie wrinkled her nose, unimpressed at the attempted wit.

"Is this where your father worked?" Reitz crossed to a desk beneath several sagging bookshelves wedged in a corner by a window looking out on an airshaft. An Underwood typewriter sat covered in the exact middle of the desk. The desk was clean and ready, as if its user was expected momentarily.

"That's where he wrote his books!" Sylvie said proudly.

"We were always getting chased out," Connie said.

"Not always," her sister said.

The fingers of Reitz' good hand slowly moved along the leather-bound volumes: Gibbons, Wells, Plutarch, Voltaire. He looked out the window. The airshaft echoed with a scratchy phonograph recording of Caruso's bell-like tenor, competing with a radio tuned to Harry James. A child laughed, another cried, an elderly women gibbered angrily in Italian. He looked down at the desk, again, admiringly, brought his fingers close to the typewriter keys, couldn't bring himself to actually touch them.

"I don't see any of your father's books."

"Mom keeps those in her room," Little Sylvie said.

Not too far off, he could hear church bells begin to chime.

"'Go in your room and be quiet!'" This from Connie. "'Daddy has to work tonight.' How can you be quiet?

We're just in the next room! If you breathed, mom'd come in to hush us!"

"She exaggerates," Sylvie said.

Connie responded by blowing a raspberry.

"And she's rude."

"A buster," Reitz concluded.

"A-men!" Sylvie said.

The woman was standing in the kitchen doorway. She was just a few years younger than her husband which put her in her late thirties, pleasant faced more than pretty. She had a soft, pillowy face, was a bit thick about the middle. Like her husband. For a moment, Reitz could picture Tommy DiFeo and his wife walking away side by side: two peas in a pod.

Again, he thought of his own wife and felt a pang.

"Tommy says I should be extra nice to you," Eve DiFeo said. "For bringing me this." She held up the sheets of paper from the envelope.

"You read it already?"

"Just the beginning."

"Well, you have been extra nice. You and your daughters."

The woman looked skeptically at her daughters.

Reitz pointed off in the direction of the tolling bells. "I should let you get on to church."

"I wish you'd — ." She stopped, considered a moment. "Would you like to come to mass with us?"

"I'm not Catholic."

"That doesn't matter."

"Only if it's all right with the ladies." He turned a beseeching look on the girls.

"Let him sit next to Sylvie," Connie said with a nasty curl to her lips. "She's the one who's all moonie over him!"

"Shut—*up!*" her older sister barked, punctuating the command with a punch to her sister's arm.

"Does that mean it's all right?" Alvin Reitz asked.

Eve DiFeo's head wagged with motherly exasperation. "Close enough."

"I'm sorry. Did I wake you?"

"Oh, no. Was I dozing off?" Reitz pulled himself upright on the bench, rubbed his eyes with his good hand. "Boy, oh, boy…" He shook his head, surprised at himself.

"You said you'd been traveling," the woman said. "You must be tired. I should've let you sleep."

Reitz smiled. "It's not that. Believe me." His eyes flicked to the achingly blue sky with just enough cotton puff clouds to make it a perfect picture. "It's just such...well, this day..."

On the south side of Clifton Avenue stood the narrow, drab stone and brick tenements of Newark's North Ward, their faces crisscrossed with rusting fire escapes, and zebra-striped with grime and coal soot. Just a little further along was the Municipal Bathhouse, an oppressive pile of brick that seemed to have been designed by the same sensibility that had designed Rahway Prison.

But the rambling miles of Branch Brook Park began on the north side of Clifton Avenue, and with the park benches faced away from the street, Reitz could easily forget – especially on just such a day — the tenements and bathhouse and the North Ward and the city beyond.

The sun was bright and warm enough to take the edge off the November chill, giving the air a clean, bracing taste. The barren trees of the park, and the brittle fallen leaves that carpeted the playground were imbued with a warm, amber glow. Children laughed and called out, scampered back and forth across the swings and jungle gym, skipping through the wind-piled mounds of leaves like a pack of monkeys. At the bocce courts on the far side of the playground, grave-faced, walnut-hided old Italian men sent wooden balls caroming off each other with quiet clicks.

What made that all such a lullaby was more than ignoring the gritty city behind them. It was something Reitz would not share with the woman which was this: The better part of his three weeks of traveling had been spent on a Liberty ship, part of a westbound OB convoy crossing the North Atlantic. Above decks had been sheathed in ice and whipped by Arctic winter gales which meant that Reitz and a few hundred other men – most of them injured as well — spent the trip cooped up below decks where the odor of fuel oil and men's bodies battled with the smell of vomit. When Reitz thought back to that voyage, the only picture that came to mind was him on his knees on the rolling deck with his head in a fire bucket.

That now felt a thousand years ago, and, instead, here was this brilliant, brilliant day. It had not taken long sitting on a bench next to Eve DiFeo, a loving sun and clean air on his face, for Reitz to begin slumping on the bench, his head beginning to drop forward.

"Mr. Reitz! Push me!" Little Sylvie was on a swing, kicking her feet anxiously. "Please, Mr. Reitz!"

"It's lieutenant!" Connie corrected from her perch atop the jungle gym. "And how's he gonna push you with a busted arm?"

"Why don't you two push each other?" their mother suggested. "Take turns."

"She can push herself," Connie snapped. Then she said something directed toward her sister Reitz couldn't quite hear. The only words he picked out were, "lovey-dovey," which – along with whatever else Connie had said – stung Sylvie like a tack on her swing seat. She vaulted to her feet and scrambled up the jungle gym with homicidal intent rage on her face.

"Be nice!" Eve DiFeo commanded. "Be-have!" "They really do love each other," she said to Reitz. "Really."

"I'm sure."

"I keep telling myself that, anyway. Do you have children?"

"Two boys and a girl. I've never seen the baby; she was born a month after my last leave."

"When was that? When you were home?"

"Last year. October."

A look on her face, like a silent, sympathetic sigh. "Have another?" She held out the small white box containing several dolci – Italian sweet pastry she had bought at a pasticerria on their way to the park.

"Thank you, no."

"Just before the war, Tommy and I had been looking for a house," she said. "Over in Bloomfield. That's not far from here, just a few miles. All we'd have to do is hop the streetcar to come back and see our people. It's very nice there. No walk-ups, no people piled on top of each other. Wide streets with trees. There's a green in the center of town and a band plays music there in the summer. Tommy had made enough money off his last book…not much, but enough for a down payment. But when I thought about moving…" She nodded at her daughters, Connie still teasing, Sylvie still giving chase ("I'm gonna kill you, I swear!"). "Sometimes I think I'd miss this."

"What makes you think it'd be different there?"

She shrugged. "None of my people has ever had a house. Tommy's, either. But it is nice there. I work out there now, in Bloomfield. GE has a factory there that makes parts for gun turrets on bombers."

"Rosie the Riveter."

She smiled self-consciously. "I'm making enough now that between that and Tommy's book money, and his allotment, I could probably get a house on my own. Only there's no houses anywhere these days. Even if I could find one..." She bowed her head. "I wouldn't want to do it until Tommy came home. He should come back to a house he knows."

She brought her face back up and Reitz was struck by the way the sun brought its warm glow to her round cheeks.

She peeked under the cover of the pastry box, almost convinced herself to close it, then quickly reached in with two gloved fingers and pinched off a piece of golden sponge cake.

Reitz smiled, turned back to his view of the park. Children. Mothers and grandmothers. The only men were old men. For a moment, a shadow of melancholia passed over his heart.

"Are you a historian like Tommy?"

"Not exactly. I'm — ..." He winced internally at the presumptuousness of the word, "artist." "I make pictures. Mostly, I draw. I paint when there's time."

"You make pictures?"

"Before Normandy, the Army had me painting watercolors of the landing beaches, the way they'd look to the coxswains that would be steering the landing craft. They'd study them so they'd know what the shore was going to look like when they went in."

"What do they have you doing now?"

"Now they just want me to draw what I see. And paint. For historical purposes."

"A soldier artist!" she marveled.

"Something like that. They have a lot of people in the field, the Army, doing what I do. People who paint and draw, photographers, guys with 16 mm movie cameras, writers —"

"Like Tommy."

"Yes."

"Why? What's it all for?"

Reitz shrugged. "Posterity. Maybe they think they'll learn something."

"Will they?"

"I doubt it."

She pinched off another piece of golden cake. "I wish you'd take some of this before I eat it all myself."

He did.

"What did you do before the war?" she asked. "Draw?"

With some self-conscious throat-clearing he said, "I was in advertising. Pieces for magazines, newspapers."

"Something I might have seen?"

"I'm afraid so. 'Smart men brace up with The Bracer! With Lastex yarn!'"

"'The Bracer?'"

"It was kind of a men's girdle. Only you couldn't call it a girdle if you wanted men to buy it."

"And now you're drawing —"

"Not too much." He wiggled the fingertips extending from the end of the cast.

"Will you be able to…?"

"The doctors say it'll be ok. We'll see."

She smiled mischievously. "Tommy said for me to ask you how it happened. He told me not to believe the first thing you said because that would probably be a lie."

"It would've been."

"So?"

He fidgeted. "You don't want to hear this."

"Tommy seems to think I would."

"Now I know where Connie gets it. Your husband's a buster, too."

"Well?"

"It's stupid."

"That's the impression he gave."

Reitz took a deep breath, couldn't help smiling himself. "I slipped on a puddle of pee in the latrine getting off the toilet."

Her gloved hand came up to cover her mouth, but it didn't do much to quiet her laugh. "Do they give you a Purple Heart for that?"

"It's a new award, just for me: the Black-and-Blue Buttock."

She no longer bothered to cover her mouth.

He thought her laugh – any woman's laugh – a beautiful, beautiful thing to hear, a sound that made the day complete.

Sylvie and Connie walked ahead of them as they headed back to their walk-up. Reitz could understand Eve DiFeo's desire to leave the neighborhood: the cramped, century-old, shoulder-to-shoulder tenements with a half-dozen families on each floor sharing a single hallway toilet; children dodging cars on the bricktop streets that served as their front yard. And yet, he could see her desire to stay, as well: she seemed to know everyone she passed by name, shopkeep and neighbor, child and adult, and they all knew her name, and asked with sincere care if there'd been any new word from her husband.

They stopped at the stoop of her building. Reitz gave the girls a nickel each to buy candied apples from the fruit store a few doors down.

"Is it like this where you're from?" Eve DiFeo asked.

"We were in Chicago until I got drafted. Then when I shipped out, Jill went home to be close to her folks. Lincoln City, Indiana. It's about forty miles from Evansville." He might just as well have told her he was from one of the moons of Jupiter. "It's a lot smaller. I think I passed more people between here and the park then there are in the whole town."

She laughed. "Where are they sending you?"

"Atlantic City. They tell me that a lot of the hotels have been converted to hospitals. As soon as my arm's better, they want me to stay on there and —"

"Make pictures."

He nodded.

"Mrs. D'Alaqua – she's one of the ladies in my building – she has a son down there." Her face clouded. "She's been down to see him. He lost a leg at Anzio."

"I'm sorry."

"She says that's mostly what they have down there. Boys who've lost legs. Arms. Boys who are paralyzed. Boys who've been burned. Sometimes…" She frowned. "Sometimes I think they keep them down there so they're out of sight." She faced him. "Tommy says he's being transferred."

"Yes."

"He says he can't say where exactly he's going. Just that it's up on the Continent. Some unit that used to be from New Jersey, he says."

"It used to be a National Guard outfit," Reitz said. "It makes a kind of Army sense. They think that since the unit used to be based in New Jersey, and that Tommy's from Jersey…"

"That doesn't make sense to you?"

"They've been in action since late June. By now, I doubt there's any more men from Jersey in that outfit than there are in any other outfit."

Now it was her turn for a shadow to pass over her heart.

He looked to lighten the moment. "Is the story true, the one Tommy told me about what happened after he enlisted? When they went to classify him?"

The shadow passed; the glowing cheeks again pulled up in a smile as she nodded. "A doctorate in history, three published books, and this sergeant told him, 'If you can write books, you must be able to type,' and they sent him to clerical school."

"See what I mean about the Army?"

They both laughed.

Reitz looked at his watch. "I have to be going. I have a train."

"Is Tommy safe? I mean, where he's going?"

Reitz smiled comfortingly. "With all respect, Eve, Tommy is no soldier. He sits with men behind the lines, asks them questions, they tell him their stories. Usually, he's so far from the front that even if they were pounding away at each other with Big Berthas, he wouldn't hear it. He'll be fine."

"Thank you for coming by, Lieutenant. Tommy calls you, 'Al,' right?"

"Al."

"Well, Al, do you think you'll be able to get yourself free and get back to — . Where was it? In Indiana?"

"Lincoln City. No, it looks like it'll be a while before I can get a long enough leave to make the trip. And with the kids, travel the way it is, there's no way it looks like she'll be able to come down."

"I'm sorry. That's a shame." A moment of thought. "Atlantic City's not far by train. If you ever have a weekend leave and want a home-cooked meal…"

"That's very sweet of you, Eve. Thank you."

"Girls, come over here and say goodbye to the lieutenant!"

Sylvie held out her little gloved hand and Reitz bowed in a gentlemanly fashion which seemed to thrill the girl no end. Then he turned to Connie and dropped to one knee.

"Coco, I was telling your mother that just after I went away, my wife had a baby girl. When she grows up, I hope she's just like you. She may give me nothing but headaches, but I'll never have to worry about whether or not she can take care of herself."

She tried not to smile but couldn't quite hide it. Slowly, her hand came up.

There was no conscious thought of it: he didn't even remember doing it. He suddenly found himself holding the girl to him in as much of a hug as he could manage with his one good arm. She did not fight him. He felt the small, dear body against him and his eyes began to sting. He pushed himself away, put a fingertip to his eyes to clear them. "I'm sorry." To no one in particular; to all of them.

"Do you have to be in Atlantic City by a certain time?" Eve DiFeo asked. "Would you girls mind if the lieutenant stayed for dinner? We eat early on Sunday," she explained to Reitz. "You could still catch an evening train and be there by tonight."

"Only if it's ok with the ladies."

Little Sylvie smiled, and Connie took his hand as if she thought it was a chore. "Come on," she grumped and led him up the stairs and through the front doors.

POSTMORTEM

"A world bereft of radical significance is not long tolerated; it leaves men radically unstable, so that they will seize at any myth or pseudomyth that is offered."

Philip Wheelwright,
"Poetry, Myth, and Reality"

I WAS BAPTIZED and raised Catholic. I attended parochial school up through the middle of fifth grade, sang soprano in the choir of my parish church, even sang the midnight High Mass for the bishop one Christmas. I dutifully contributed money to foreign missions dedicated to redeeming the souls of pagan babies, and bought religious items at the annual icon sale (including an eight-inch-high Holy Family number with a secret compartment containing a glow-in-the-dark rosary). I was so committed to the letter of Catholicism – or at least the knuckle-wrapping, cheek-twisting, hair-pulling catechism served up by the nuns in my schools – that even scratching an innocent itch "down there" moved me to whisper a heartfelt Act of Contrition and light a couple of candles in church.

At what point along my lifeline that sort of dedication to the faith faded, I couldn't tell you, but, along with my ability to sing soprano, fade it most definitely did. There was no epiphany of disbelief, just a slow erosion, things nibbling away at my Catholic conviction bit by bit. Like the time a nun explained away UFOs by saying they might be angels (an odd reflection: an 11-year-old is more apt to believe in the reality of flying saucers than angels). Or my gradual dawning that the adoption of Saturday night Mass had more to do with Catholics not wanting to get up on Sunday morning than as a considerate bow to "those who may have conflicting obligations on the Sabbath." Or the time I puzzled over why the monsignor was rushing so quickly through one of those Saturday night masses like a tobacco auctioneer until I realized Notre Dame basketball was on TV in forty-five minutes. One's faith does begin to falter when one sees the dedication of the clergy waver under an early tip-off time.

I started wondering if how nicely I dressed for church was really such a big deal to God because the nuns and my mother seemed to think so; or if God really cared if I'd had a couple of eggs for breakfast less than an hour before receiving Communion. There was a point where it seemed to me God cared more about me wearing a tie in his house than saving my father's life.

My father passed away at age forty-nine from a form of leukemia. I was thirteen.

It was a gray day when we put my father in the ground, overcast, a little chilly. That's how I remember it, but maybe all burials are remembered that way.

My mother had sent me back to the limo while she stood by the grave to see him laid down. The priest who'd led us in the graveside prayers followed me. I was quick stepping to the car, crying, wanting to be done crying, unable to stop crying, and he was hurrying after me offering solace. His comforting thought for the day was something about me having to believe there was some kind of reason behind all this; a *purpose*.

As if believing so would've made it hurt any less.

One of my ex-girlfriends would've laughed. Karmic justice, she would've called it.

She always thought me a dedicated cynic. I did have a rather nasty predisposition in the days we were together to pooh-pooh anything requiring an element of faith, whether it was UFOs or angels or the edibility of sushi. I don't think you have to be a $100 an hour shrink to figure that since my Catholic God had let me down in my youth with the death of my father, over the years I'd gotten to the point where I didn't think much of anybody else's God either, or *any* kind of faith for that matter. Consequently, she would've gotten a hoot and a half out of me taking a job which would *force* me to wrestle a choke collar on my more skeptical penchants.

It was autumn and an agent friend of mine called asking if I knew any non-fiction writers with an interest in the paranormal. She had a possible project for them. It seems a couple she knew thought they were having some sort of communication with The Beyond — .

"You're kidding."

"That's what they say."

"You mean like ghosts?"

"Well, they're not seeing ghosts, but that *kind* of thing."

"You're *kidding*."

The couple was looking for somebody, preferably a writer who already believed in that *kind* of thing, to help them dope out a proposal for a book about their experiences. Assuming a publisher expressed an interest in the proposal, the writer would then, presumably, help them with the actual writing of the book.

"Ghosts?"

"*Not* ghosts. *Communications!*"

I said I didn't know anybody.

She mentioned how much money the couple was offering for just the proposal.

I said, "Hmmm."

Up to that point in what was laughingly passing for my "writing career" (and at that time, it most assuredly deserved those quotation marks) I'd had no particular interest in non-fiction. And – without conceding my ex's indictment of my spiritual tunnel vision – even less in supposedly true ghost stories.

But I did have an interest in getting published and getting those quotes off from around "writing career." I agreed with the agent there was definitely a market for this sort of thing. I was also in a new relationship and it was working well enough that me and my significant other had become engaged just a few weeks before. Money being what it was (or rather, wasn't) in both our families, my fiancée and I were going to have to foot the bill for the wedding ourselves. The amount the agent mentioned would cover a nice piece of it.

"Hell," I told her, "for that kind of money, *I'm* interested!"

I also did have a certain honest curiosity. The whole affair sounded like the kind of thing you only saw in stuff like *The Haunting, Poltergeist, The House On Haunted Hill.* You know: *X-Files* stuff. Only this was real life. Committed skeptic or not, it was hard to resist the opportunity to get a peek at something like this.

However, after the agent filled me in on some of the details, this business hardly seemed like a lark. The "communications" this couple claimed to be having were with the spirit of their dead son. Several years earlier, after battling depression for some time, he'd committed suicide at the age of twenty-one just a few days before Christmas. Nope, not sounding like much of a lark at all.

Let's call them Joe and Mary Davidson, and the son: Samuel.

The Davidsons sent the agent some material to forward to me so I could make a more informed decision about whether or not this was something I wanted to get involved in (as well as a more informed decision about whether or not I thought this was something I could carry off). This was providing that, in the end, they wanted me involved at all. The Davidsons' package contained a diary Joe Davidson had kept of his and his wife's supposed contacts with the spirit of their son, and transcripts of several sessions they'd had with mediums.

These "contacts" were nothing as blatant as apparitions or disembodied voices. The agent had been right: no ghosts. I guess you'd describe these events as more symbolic in nature: coming across Prince's "When Doves Cry" video on TV (the Davidsons associated Samuel with doves); or seeing a dove outside the window or set down on a golf green while they'd been thinking of him; someone resembling Samuel wearing a shirt that was twin to his favorite shirt; a caller on Samuel's phone asking for him after he'd died. These were the kinds of incidents the Davidsons considered messages from their deceased son.

There were also a few more truly macabre claims, the most patently ghostly of them being episodes of mysterious flashings of the dining room lights.

Besides Joe Davidson's diary, also enclosed were two books: *Stephen Lives! My Son Stephen: His Life, Suicide, and Afterlife,* by Anne Puryear, who'd lost her 15-year-old son to suicide and claimed to have communication with his spirit; and *Hello From Heaven! A New Field of Research – After-Death Communication – Confirms That Life and Love Are Eternal,* by Bill and Judy Guggenheim, a compilation of accounts by people claiming to have experienced some form of "ADC" (the Guggenheims' tag for "After-Death Communication").

Even before I'd opened up the package from the agent, I'd pretty well written off the whole crowd – the Davidsons, Puryear, the Guggenheims, and the Guggenheims' subjects – as loons (so much for journalistic objectivity). But the more I read, the harder it was to write them off completely.

Oh, it had nothing to do with believing or disbelieving them. Granted, I couldn't account for everything these people said they'd seen, felt, and heard, although – in my typically close-minded fashion – not for one second did I think they were getting messages from

The Other Side. No, the kicker for me was that however unreal their experiences may have been, the pain behind them was obviously very, *very* real, and that pain I couldn't dismiss.

They were all – the Davidsons as well as the people in the books – trying to cope with monumental emotional traumas. Loved ones had been lost, often before what one would judge to be "their time," often abruptly, leaving gaping, aching wounds in psyches and hearts. Accidents, suicides, disease – the pages in my hands were a catalogue of personal catastrophe and misery, of the unfairness of lives incomplete.

The survivors were looking – *desperately* looking, I thought – for an anesthetic. If they'd been talking about flying saucers I could've laughed. I couldn't laugh at someone talking about losing a friend, a parent, a child, even if, in the same breath, they were talking about ghosts and "ADCs."

I couldn't laugh or dismiss it because I'd felt the same gut-wrenching pain they'd felt, and the same angry sense of unfairness, and the same unfillable void in my heart when my father had died.

And the hunger to fill that void?

I feel it still.

After I read the Davidsons' material I sent them writing samples and a proposal for the book as I'd envisioned it. They were looking for something, in their words, to "communicate the message of comfort" they were getting from Samuel's contacts. I took that to mean a book – if it became a book – that would end up on the same bookstore shelf next to titles like Puryear's and the Guggenheims' and I didn't want that. I wanted to be published, yes, but from a point of professional survival I thought a reputation as a guy who wrote airy-fairy spooky-cooky true-life tales of the paranormal would be a career-killer for someone aspiring to work that was more "serious." And, on a personal level, I didn't want anybody writing *me* off as a loon the way I'd done to Puryear et al.

So, I pitched the kind of project I thought would maintain a certain – and admittedly presumptuous – literary integrity, and which I also hoped would still make an interesting read. I wanted a book looking critically at the Davidsons' story, one that would challenge their assumptions, question their experiences, and leave the question of "is it or isn't it real?" something for the reader to answer.

A part of me hoped my samples and the pitch would convince them I was wrong for the job. The closer our dialogue came to making this thing happen, the more reluctant I felt about poking around in their personal tragedy, especially for the mercenary purpose of getting a first published credit.

But they liked my stuff.

We met for the first time in November of that year, just a few weeks short of the anniversary of Samuel's death.

It was cold that day, colder than I remembered it usually being for that time of the year. Still, I decided to walk from my office on 42nd Street up to their apartment in a well-moneyed part of uptown Manhattan. I was going to have a pitch to make and a sale to close; the walk would give me time to organize my thoughts. And, it's not every day you get to visit a haunted house (well, haunted co-op, actually); one needs a little time to psychologically gear up for that.

Joe Davidson met me at the door of their apartment and led me into the living room. Probably from watching *Rosemary's Baby* too many times I'd expected to find a dark, shadowy place populated with glum-faced, hollow-voiced people enveloped in grief behind closed, dark drapes and so on and so forth. You know; a real urban gothic theme. But the Davidson place, which took up the whole floor of the building, was spacious, airy, pleasantly bright, done in light colors, the walls heavily decorated with an entertaining variety of artwork. There was obviously serious money here, but, at the same time, there was nothing gaudy or overbearing about the place or its resident who was neither glum-faced nor hollow-voiced. Somewhere in his sixties, I guessed, Joe was a soft-spoken, warm and genial you-must-be-Bill-come-on-in-and-have-a-seat kind of guy.

In the living room by the fireplace I noted a low, glass table supporting a number of crystal sculptures, a number of them being various kinds of birds. I wondered if they were supposed to be doves. In a corner of the room was a grand piano, the lid covered in a forest of family pictures including several of Samuel.

Among the paintings on the walls were two small canvases by Samuel. My grasp of formal art aestheticism wouldn't quite fill a thimble, but I liked the simple balance of the composition and colors in these simple renderings.

For a while, it was just Joe and me. He asked if I'd had a chance to look over the material he'd sent over, and when I said yes he asked what I thought.

"Frankly," I said to him, "I don't know what to make of it," which may have been a bit of a gutless waffle, but it was also sort of true.

He nodded and seemed unsurprised, probably knowing this was my diplomatic way of saying, "Gimme a break."

We chatted vaguely about the proposed book until a little later when Mary came home. Stout but handsome, she seemed much younger than Joe. Her voice was stronger, firmer, and where Joe moved with an almost deliberate delicateness, Mary bustled about quickly and decisively. Like Joe, she was immediately friendly, but her conversation – always unfailingly polite and warm – was more direct and quickly to the point.

Over the next hour or so, we exchanged thoughts about the project. I was struck at the outset by their awareness of how loopy their story sounded to others; loopy enough to have cost them several friendships. They knew no one who hadn't experienced what they had could ever wholly believe it. They told me even after having long accepted the reality of these events, they themselves didn't necessarily believe it *all*, and continued to challenge each new occurrence, evaluating it before deciding what was really a communication from Samuel, and what was just a coincidence and/or wishful thinking.

At the same time, they spoke of Samuel's communications with a stunning nonchalance, making no attempt to hype me on the extraordinary nature of these events. It was my prejudices coming into play which had had me expecting them to describe what they had been experiencing in awed and hushed tones (remember Beatrice Straight in *Poltergeist?* Like that). They simply related what, to them, had become over several years a regular – albeit remarkable – part of their world. They might just as well have been being visited by a clever squirrel who'd learned to stand up and beg to get a peanut; something unusual, but not unnatural.

I don't know how you compare losing a father to losing a son (and it may be ludicrous to even make such a comparison), but I know what it's like to lose someone you love; I know that, like a deep wound, it may heal but it will never stop hurting; and I know it enough to recognize the scars in others. That kind of hurt was still there with the Davidsons, even several years after

Samuel's death, and it was still close enough to the surface that, at one point, when talking about Samuel, Mary's eyes began to tear up. I also recognized the signs clearly enough to feel a kinship with them, and to feel more than a twinge of guilt at initially having been so – covertly – dismissive of them.

These were not people, as I had prematurely feared, adrift and drowning in grief, barely muddling through one moping day after another. They were lively, pleasant, vital.

And why not? Samuel was still alive for them! More, it was not the Samuel they had known in this life: depressive and pained. This was a Samuel freed from his demons.

"I'm not afraid to die," Mary said to me in her forthright way. "Joe's not afraid to die. We're not afraid to die. We know someone who loves us is waiting for us. We know there's something else."

That comfort, they told me, was what they wanted to share in their hoped-for book. God knows it wasn't for money (one look around that apartment and you knew they didn't need the money). Like all True Believers, they thought they'd found an answer, and wanted to share that answer and the healing power they believed it would bring to others similarly wounded by loss. They had suffered through their long, dark night of the soul, and the message Joe and Mary Davidson had come out of it with and wanted to share was that their long dark night had come to an end.

I walked the forty blocks from the Davidson's down to Penn Station where I'd board a train to take me across the Hudson and home. I needed the time in the crisp, autumn night air to think.

Even before meeting them I'd categorized the Davidson story as something not believable, but now I'd been thrown by the obvious fact these were not candidates for a rousing rondelle with Oprah. These were white collar professionals, well-educated, sharp, and savvy. Sitting there with them, faced with that unblinking conviction of theirs and the utterly reasonable manner they'd presented it to me, I *had* to think, "Well *something* is touching these people!"

So why not the spirit of their dead son?

On the walk to my train, even that little bit of wavering couldn't hold up against the obvious. I had sat in the home where Samuel's spirit had, supposedly, been visiting for years. In Joe's diary I'd read of flashing dining room lights, bizarre phone calls, inexplicable tinklings of wind chimes.

I'd sat with the Davidsons for about an hour discussing the world of these other-worldly visitations, and not once in that time had the lights flashed or the wind chimes chimed. If ever there had been a time for Samuel to send a message, I would have thought that to be the time.

A part of me – the hungry, inner part I prefer to ignore most of the time, the I-dare-you-to-be-real part – wanted to see those dining room lights flash. But the truth I've come to realize, with some sadness, I must say, is that even if Samuel had appeared in front of me in some ectoplasmic state, I'd still have found some reason to disbelieve it. I'd have called it induced hysteria, suggestion, an hallucination, something, *anything*, because of part of me would've kept declaring, "This *can't* be!"

Later, doing some "homework" for the project, I read a passage in Episcopal Bishop John Shelby Spong's *Liberating the Gospels* which hit the problem on the head for me. Bishop Spong wrote of his own similar dilemma, of how he, as both a Christian and a theologic scholar, felt confronting the supernatural events of The Bible:

"No matter how hard I try, I cannot bend
my mind into a first-century pretzel. I
cannot turn my postmodern mind into a
premodern shape. I cannot believe in my
heart something my mind rejects."

As I kept running the evening over and over in my
mind, I had to acknowledge I'd gone up to the Davidsons
not on an objective search for facts, but as a narrow-
minded twit looking for confirmation of my prejudices
and a quick paycheck. But, even conceding that, I hadn't
had to look very hard. For instance…

At one point in the conversation Mary had said the
reason more people couldn't communicate with the
spiritual plane the way she and Joe did with Samuel was
because people didn't allow themselves to be open to
such contacts.

Though I hadn't said anything aloud – and granting
most people (like me) are not open even to the *idea* of
paranormal phenomena – that was a point I had no
problem, reservations, or guilt about pooh-poohing. I've
never seen people as open and vulnerable as they are at
the moment of a loved one's death. Grief eclipses all the
usual restraints: reason, logic, social inhibition. I've seen
people throw themselves across bodies lying in open

caskets, shouting at the deceased, praying aloud hysterically for the fact of death to be undone.

I wanted my father back so badly I kept hoping – in what I think is a common funeral fantasy – he'd sit up in that coffin and say it was a mistake, a bad joke, a dream.

I never heard a message. Not then, nor in the over forty years since we buried him.

Another for-example…

Joe had spoken of several séances he and his wife had attended. He had told me about one medium who had, on just meeting him, correctly revealed Joe had had a different name when he was younger, and that his family had been immigrants. To Joe, this was evidence of the medium's extrasensory ability.

But…

When Joe speaks, you can hear a New York Jewish cadence. It wouldn't be unreasonable to assume (certainly I had no trouble assuming) a man of his age, with his accent, was from a family which had emigrated from eastern Europe probably during the large European immigration waves in the years before and just after World War II. On that basis, it would be a pretty good bet the family's eastern European name had been changed (not too many Poles or Slavs named Davidson) when immigrants were more concerned about Americanizing than in preserving their ethnic heritage (and, indeed, Joe's family had changed their name from the original Russian).

Am I trying too hard to pooh-pooh?

A friend of mine is married to a Cuban woman who learned some basic palmistry from the older women in her family. Olga is not a boardwalk fortune teller but a paralegal and a pretty good one. She once "read" my palm and was astoundingly on the money about so many things I had to do what I had briefly done in the Davidson house: start wondering.

However, Olga made no pretense that clairvoyance or any other paranormality was at work. It was simple – but extremely shrewd – observation: condition of the fingers, the nails, skin of the hands, careful study not just of the hand but of the face ("You have concerns; you're not sleeping well" – because I had shadows under my eyes). She was also picking up tension in the hand when she'd voice a "reading," as well as other sometimes subtle, unconscious reactions – what gamblers and con men refer to as a "tell" – I'd had to things she said. A good palmist, I learned, is part detective, part human polygraph.

All this I got from somebody who only occasionally did this sort of thing for fun. There are those who do it for a living.

After my meeting with the Davidsons, I heard from my agent that Joe and Mary were still interested in going forward with the project with me but some time would probably pass while a formal agreement was hammered out. I decided to use that time doing some homework. Whatever my personal feelings and prejudices were, the Davidsons were opening up a very personal part of themselves to me. I owed it to them to do due diligence.

First, I went back to Joe's diary and the transcripts he'd sent me of six séances by four different mediums. I'm not looking to embarrass or get into a feud with anybody so I'm not going to mention names, but I will say that you could find some of these mediums' names on the shelves at Barnes & Noble, hear about them appearing on TV, see ads for them appearing at major live events. At least some of them are ranked as the best for this sort of thing.

Yet I couldn't find in my reading of the transcripts the same sense of certainty and confirmation the Davidsons had found for what they were experiencing. The bulk of each reading was, in my judgment, insubstantial; shockingly so, considering how much faith Joe and Mary had in these people.

There were statements concerning Samuel's supposed state of mind, his feelings about family members and relatives...all so vague and subjective in nature it would be hard for a family member *not* to have found an element of truth to them. There had also been a number of predictions often also vague, and, in terms of time frame, frequently open-ended. With such elastic parameters, eventually *something* would come to pass which could be interpreted as fitting the bill.

For example, the first medium the Davidsons sat with reported Samuel had said something about somebody in the family going north which the Davidsons assumed referred to Samuel's half-brother's attendance at a university reunion in New England. But think about it: it's a fuzzy enough statement to cover anything from the half-brother's trip to a subway ride to Yankee Stadium.

When the mediums tried for something more specific, to me they appeared – to crib from Perry Mason – to be "leading the witness." Some more for-example's...

According to Joe's diary, the Davidsons had their first session with a medium a little over a year after Samuel's death. In the transcript of the reading, the medium states that the deceased was in his twenties or thirties, a pretty wide spread easily covering the age of a child from someone in the Davidsons' age bracket.

The Davidsons were asked who in the family played cards? Who smoked? Probability would weigh in that *somebody* in the family played cards; *somebody* smoked.

The medium said Samuel believed they would soon be traveling "over water" and – with a question mark at the end – put out "Europe." The Davidsons are quite well-to-do, they travel somewhere almost every year. An overseas trip wouldn't be much of a reach.

But most striking to me was that Samuel's suicide was never made manifest. The medium "knew" Samuel was dead, but never hinted at that most salient fact: *how* he died.

Then there were curios from a session with another medium visited seven months later.

The medium asked – *asked*, mind you – if Joe and Mary had a son who had died. Not a statement, but a question asked to a couple probably too old to have living parents, who had obviously come to speak to the spirit of someone whose loss troubled them enough to seek out a medium. A reasonable guess.

After the medium had been made aware the Davidsons had lost a son, he asked if the boy had taken drugs or was depressed: again, not statements but questions. A young death would reasonably indicate an unnatural death, and how much of a reach to guess at drugs? And if he was using drugs, how much further a reach to assume he might have emotional problems?

Most saliently, like the first medium, this second communicator made no statement indicating an awareness of the most trenchant aspect of Samuel's death: that it was a suicide.

The Davidsons visited this same medium two days later, and the same trawling pattern which had troubled me in the transcript of the first session was still there. Now knowing Samuel took drugs and suffered from depression, the medium *asks* (again, no definitive statement) if their son had been taking antidepressants.

Having gotten an affirmative answer, the medium now goes off into what I interpreted as logical extrapolations, saying how Samuel took more of his prescribed drugs than he should have, that he suffered from mood swings and had difficulties socializing, and that he'd suffered emotional problems since childhood.

And, only *after* having established that Samuel had been treated for depression does the medium make any reference to suicide, and even then only in vague terms saying the Davidsons' boy had taken "control of his life."

The following summer, the Davidsons visited a third medium. According to the transcript, it seemed the medium wasn't even sure he was dealing with a male spirit, saying there were several entities present, both male and female. Afterward came the trawling I was now coming to consider characteristic of these sessions.

It was hard to be impressed by such supposedly paranormal insights as the medium stating that someone had died (who visits a medium to talk to the living?), that the Davidsons were his parents (in light of their obvious age, hardly a revelation), and that the deceased had had health trouble (he was, after all, deceased). Not only did this medium not initially sense a suicide, but he went as far as to propose a brain tumor. And all these statements came in the form of questions.

After the Davidsons explain Samuel had had a mental illness, the medium tries to reconcile this with his brain tumor revelation saying Samuel's spirit is explaining to him that his problem "affects my head." From there, the medium tells the Davidsons Samuel was not a happy person and that he often made his problems worse.

Several weeks later, the Davidsons went back to the second medium. Joe was particularly impressed on this visitation that the medium could divine Joe had been married once before. The exchange came up after Joe mentioned a note he'd put on someone's photograph. But this remarkable revelation only came about after what seemed like a game of Twenty Questions.

The medium asked if the photograph was of a friend.

Joe told him no.

A relative?

No.

A woman?

Yes.

His sister?

No.

Was it someone very close to Joe?

At one time, yes, Joe answers.

A few more Q & As follow and only then does the medium shock Joe by telling him the woman was his first wife. Still, as with Samuel, the medium could not immediately sense Joe's previous spouse had committed suicide. Instead, the Q & A resumes with the medium asking if she'd been on drugs. Pills? Had she killed herself with pills?

That fall, the Davidsons went to a fourth medium who impressed them when early in the session he stated Samuel hadn't died of an illness (which is not quite as impressive considering the Davidsons had already told him Samuel had died at twenty-one), but he couldn't sense the cause of death was suicide.

The medium's other insights were no less unimpressive, like the one where he asked if these two well-to-do Manhattanites lived in a co-op.

A month later, the Davidsons held a phone session with still another medium.

The medium asks if Samuel had had an affinity for music. *After* he gets a yes, he says Samuel's spirit is showing him some kind of musical object "you blow on" which must take in a third to a half of the instruments in an orchestra. As it happened, Samuel had had a saxophone, although he never played. Still, give the medium a half-point.

Give him another one when he says Samuel is showing him a keyboard (remember that grand piano in the Davidsons' living room).

Then take a point away when he brings in a xylophone and put him at zero when he won't let it go, asking if maybe Samuel had had one as a child, presumably one of those ubiquitous kiddie xylophones. I took it the medium had made a wrong call and then kept at it fishing for *something* to validate the statement.

Toting it all up, it'd be easy to write off these switchboard operators to the afterlife as nothing more than good carnie acts. Except...

One of the mediums had come up with a revelation that someone in the family had a sizable collection of classical records. It was Samuel's half-brother, and if that had been a guess, it was a hell of a guess.

That paled next to the medium who'd clued into an abortion Mary'd had. And if *that* had been a guess, we're talking about the Mother of All Guesses.

That is, as I say, *if* it was a guess.

Maybe all of these mediums *were* The Real Deal; they honest-to-God (or whatever) *were* plugged into lines of communication with another plane of existence. And, maybe all the vagaries and questions and probing were part of how the system worked.

Assume there is some sort of spiritual plane; some other level of being we'd define as an afterlife. Unless it's a purely magical experience, it's possible – common sense would say damned probable – it's subject to certain laws of action much the way our more familiar corporeal universe functions under the laws of physics. Lacking first-hand observations, we have no way of knowing what those laws are, but, perhaps being what they are – whatever they are – spirit communication can only break through to our plane in unclear, intermittent signals, like getting a long-distance radio signal. Or, maybe it's like dipping into police radio bands; there's a torrent of material going here and there and it's hard to pick out the message from the one individual you want. And, of course, the willingness of the recipient might affect how well or how poorly contact is made.

A True Believer would call this an explanation; a skeptic a rationale.

If I'd been sitting in on those séances, saw the mediums at work, felt the same charged atmosphere the Davidsons had felt, sensed the same energy in the room, I might've been more open to non-skeptical explanations than I was reading about them alone in my apartment several years after the fact.

Before my meeting with the Davidsons, my agent had brought up the possibility of my attending one of those séances thinking not only would it be a good addition for the book, but also a way for me to at least partly feel what Joe and Mary had felt in those sessions.

But the Davidsons didn't go to them anymore. They'd gotten from them what they'd needed, and knew all they needed to know: the spirit of Samuel was alive and happy and in contact with them.

A number of years earlier, I had worked for a publishing company and had routinely scooped up a copy of almost every title they released while I was there, everything from a biography of Martin Buber to a coffee table book on American quilts. We had also done a fair number of volumes on mysticism, metaphysics, religion, various spiritual disciplines, etc.

In the years since I'd left the house, those books had been sitting on my shelves at home gathering dust, but now I could put them to good use. I went through them trying to find out what people knew, thought they knew, mused, surmised, and guessed about the existence and workings of an afterlife, other planes of existence, the paranormal. I also pulled out some psychology texts to see what, if any, the clinical thinking was on non-paranormal explanations for paranormal activity.

One particularly interesting line of thinking grounded the paranormal on a hybrid base of theoretical science and eastern mysticism. The writings ranged from the philosophical cosmology of the late Itzhak Bentov in his *A Cosmic Book: On the Mechanics of Creation*, to the comparatively hardcore science of Fred Alan Wolf, one-time professor of physics at San Diego State University, who, with Bob Toben, and "in conversation with theoretical physicists" (so said the cover copy) penned, *Space-Time and Beyond: Toward an Explanation of the Unexplainable.*

As I understand this particular view (and I'm not quite sure I do), paranormal phenomena – from garden variety clairvoyance to more mystical concepts like higher states of consciousness – are governed by the same physical laws at work in the universe we're more familiar with. This view contends that our inability to regularly witness paranormal phenomena, or exercise our allegedly innate capacity for it, is a product of a self-imposed separation between our material universe and its more mystical side.

Quantum physics tells us everything is a form of energy. The difference between what most of us think of as energy (say heat or light) and matter (like this book you're holding in your hand) is only that the molecules in this page are vibrating at a different frequency than the molecules in a beam of light. According to this scientific/mystic view, at a higher level of consciousness, we can plug into the energy comprising all things – including thought – at which point things paranormal become the norm.

How does this apply to death and afterlife? If all matter and energy is the same thing, and matter, as Einstein taught us, can neither be created nor destroyed, then the energy which comprises our consciousness doesn't extinguish just because our bodies cease functioning and crumble away. The collection of energy making up our thoughts, memories, personality – all those things that come together as *us* – goes on. "There is no death," write Wolf/Toben, "only a change of awareness, a change of cosmic address."

Now, there's a point in the body of scientific thought where you move from substantiated core knowledge through accepted theory to an area so speculative it shares a border with fantasy; a place where nearly anything is possible (though not necessarily probable). This scientific brand of mysticism is based substantially on elements of quantum theory, an area highly theoretical to begin with (for the record: quantum theory, and I'll quote Webster here, is "...a theory in physics based on the concept of the subdivision of radiant energy into finite quanta and applied to numerous processes involving transference or transformation of energy in an atomic or molecular scale," and no, I don't understand that what means, either).

Lord Kelvin, the mathematician and physicist, set a scientific standard in the 19th Century when he took the position that anything "real" could be measured. But mysticism and quantum theory both try to explain processes in the universe involving occurrences and/or forces which we cannot see, touch, or measure. By that token, one should be taken as seriously as the other, right?

Accepted scientific theory is an extrapolation of what we *do* know. Again, to consider quantum theory, we may be unable to look directly at atoms and how they work, but our theories on how things happen at the atomic and sub-atomic level, and how they play out in the universe, are borne out in phenomena which *are* observable, measurable, and repeatable (Hiroshima, for example, standing as grim proof that a lot of atomic theory is on the money). Those phenomena not only provide corroboration for theories about how matter and energy work but offer a substantial platform from which to launch into theories about other unobservable forces at work in the universe.

But mysticism, well, that's something else again, because, historically, its disciples have been unable to provide the same kind of firm foundation data. The paradox of mysticism based on science is that while claiming a certain scientific legitimacy, it fails the basic challenges for the scientific proving which would grant that legitimacy.

Back in the 1960s, Henry Sidgewick, a professor of philosophy at Cambridge University, and a number of associates who shared his negative opinion of the snooty way mainstream science continually dismissed the paranormal, created the Society for Psychical Research. Sidgewick & Co. wanted to explore, by scientific methods, the kinds of things science usually brushed off with a, "Bah! Humbug!" Said Sidgewick, "...there was an important body of evidence – tending on the face of it to establish the independence of soul or spirit – which modern science had simply left on one side with ignorant contempt."

But Sidgewick also allowed, "…we did not say these negative conclusions were erroneous…only…that they had been arrived at prematurely."

Too often, "scientific" testing of paranormal phenomena fell victim to the prejudices of its testers. Physicist and mathematician John Taylor, in his book, *Science and the Supernatural*, visited a number of paranormal experiments and found, time and again, testers had – sometimes unwittingly, sometimes unconsciously – compromised the objective circumstances of their experiments.

Take the case of one-time paranormal tyro Uri Geller who had made the long-since discredited claim that, among other things, he could bend spoons with the power of his mind. Geller's supposed ability was tested successfully – and inaccurately – under laboratory conditions. Taylor wondered "…how a band of parapsychologists, some of them with Ph.D.'s in physics, chemistry or mathematics, could persuade themselves that the absolute contrary to (what they know) is actually occurring?" James (The Amazing) Randi, a professional magician who was also a professional paranormal debunker, gave Taylor his answer: "Because I have seen what grown men will do to satisfy a deep need to believe." In his book's summation, Taylor quoted Sir John Eccles, Nobel Laureate in Physiology: "The mind is *the* problem in any parapsychological investigation."

Though supporters of the mystical, Wolf and Toben hit on the same problem. They point to the "…multitudes of people, culture, and institutes…" who apply themselves to studying the paranormal – everything from psychokinesis and clairvoyance to astral travel and reincarnation – and ask why science can't seem to definitively confirm or deny such phenomena. "The chief criterion of any scientific evidence is that it be repeatable and demonstrable. In other words, it must be objectively observed," they write and figure that to be the problem since so much paranormal phenomena – in their view – "..is quite subjective and depend(s) on the state of the observer."

A good example of Wolf/Toben's punch line is a chapter from *Hello From Heaven!* presenting a collection of what the Guggenheims label "sleep-state ADCs." These ADCs feature subjects who've gone to sleep, then, in some cases, awakened to experience a visitation or sign from a deceased person. Or, in other cases, they didn't wake up, but had some sort of out-of-body experience bringing them into contact with a spirit. In still other cases, the spirit of the deceased intruded into the subject's dream.

The Guggenheims say none of these are dreams – a skeptic's immediate response – but bonafide ADCs. They know this because, in part, the subjects' – and the Guggenheims – *believe* they're not dreams. Beyond that, they discount the dream possibility through some arbitrarily defined differences between dreams and ADCs, such as dreams are usually fragmented and filled with symbolism, incomplete in one way or another, and have "...a quality of unreality about them..." On the other hand, sleep-state ADCs, they write, *feel* real. They're more organized and vivid than dreams.

But science writer Gordon Rattray Taylor, in his book, *The Natural History of the Mind*, points out how powerfully vivid visions can be provoked by "...an intense need or desire for the object hallucinated..." (i.e. somebody in a desert hallucinating an oasis) including the cases of "...people who see loved ones after their death."

Taylor tells of the case of Francoise Delisle, mistress to famed English psychologist Havelock Ellis, who, after Ellis' death, swore she saw Ellis move through her room, an apparition so vivid she followed it out into her garden where it disappeared.

The Guggenheims' treatment of other ADC categories isn't any more rigorous. Throughout their book, they regularly cite "feelings" and "sensations" as a form of ADC based solely on the belief shared with their subjects that that's what they are. That such feelings could be explained as typical manifestations of grief doesn't get much serious consideration.

One category – "symbolic ADCs" – begs for trouble. Symbolic ADCs are things like rainbows, flowers, animals, and other comforting but earthly items interpreted as ADCs either because of their association with the deceased, and/or their appearance in some timely fashion. So, somebody's driving down a road, he/she sees a rainbow, this somebody *thinks* this is a message from a deceased loved one, and the Guggenheims say it is because this somebody *believes* it to be. That tens of thousands of *other* people also see the same rainbow and think of it as nothing more than a rainbow doesn't dissuade the Guggenheims from accepting this somebody's testimony that this was a message aimed right at them.

If I could put the Guggenheims and Taylor together in a point/counter-point duel, I'm sure the Guggenheims would make the case that Taylor, in the Delisle case, dismissed an authentic ADC with scientific rationalization. Taylor would probably respond to the Guggenheims were regularly misinterpreting dreams and hallucinations. And, if Itzhak Bentov could speak from The Other Side, he'd probably tell them both dreams and ADCs are part of the same energy flow occurring in higher states of consciousness.

My problem was these kinds of highly symbolic, highly subjective incidents were what made up most of Joe Davidson's diary: a song picked up on the radio or MTV Joe felt connected to Samuel; live and symbolic doves; people named Samuel or who resembled Samuel; and so on. It all seemed like stuff being granted a paranormal significance only because of the way the Davidsons interpreted it.

Joe and Mary, in our meeting, were willing to acknowledge how these signs could look like coincidences. But they believed the reason they *weren't* was what they considered to be the extraordinary frequency of occurrences.

To me, there was nothing extraordinary about it. To me, it was like suddenly realizing how many other people own a red car when *you* buy a red car. The frequency of occurrence hasn't changed; just the sensitivity to that occurrence. The phenomenon that *is* occurring happens not in the realm of the paranormal, but in the very real world of the mind. Jonathan Miller in his *The Body in Question*, put it like this: "What the mind sees is not what there is, but what it supposes there might be."

Curiously, in all the books I read which offered support of the paranormal – from the purely mystical to the quasi-scientific – death and the afterlife were, at best, only rarely mentioned. An author convinced of the whole buffet of paranormal phenomena would dedicate just a few sentences out of an entire book to what happened to a person's psychic energy during and after death. Even Evelyn Underhill's massive *Mysticism*, a classic primer on its subject for the better part of the 20th Century, gave short shrift to dying and the hereafter.

Evidently, that great mystery Death remains largely a mystery…even to mystics.

What was supposed to have been a few weeks to work out an agreement for the project stretched into months. The Davidsons were traveling for a while, then December – being the anniversary of Samuel's death – was hard on them, and, of course, there was the usual contract haggling. As frustrating as the hold-up was, it did give me more time to lay groundwork for the book.

What I was dealing with, it seemed more and more to me, was not something paranormal, mystical, or even quantum physics. It was an issue of faith. These perceived manifestations of Samuel were what the Davidsons thought they were because that's what they *believed* them to be. That's faith. And faith, as I've already pointed out, is hardly my strongpoint.

So, I brought it up with an expert.

The December after my meeting with the Davidsons, I was hunting for someone to perform my wedding and had been referred to the minister of a nearby Pentecostal church. Like myself, he was a one-time Catholic (as were, curiously, the majority of his church membership), and also like myself, of Italian extraction (for those of you whose picture of Pentecostals has been formed by cheap-shot southern-accented lampoons on TV and in the movies, this gentleman's distinctly Jerseyesque demeanor would come as a revelation). Since it had always been part of my book proposal to the Davidsons that I'd include views from clergymen, mental health professionals, and so on, I took advantage of one of our pre-nuptial sit-downs to ask the good reverend about the Davidsons.

"I'm just wondering what the Biblical view on something like this is," I asked.

He didn't hesitate in his response. "There's no way dead people can talk to live people," he said with a Jersey-flavored bluntness. "When you die, you either go up, or you go down. I'm putting it simply, but that's it."

As for what the Davidsons were going through, he said with a gentle sadness and sympathy, "That's grief."

He illustrated his point with some lines from the Old Testament. The reverend pointed to King David's mourning the death of the son he'd had by Bathsheba. The scripture reads, "…now he is dead…Can I bring him back again? I shall go to him, but he will not return to me."

Dr. Joanne McMahon taught me about "synchronicity," which she defined for me as "symbolic coincidences" – events that can have symbolic meaning without being paranormal. Like the Davidsons and their doves.

Actually, my hooking up with McMahon was something of a synchronous event in itself. A friend of mine worked for a Newark hospital and I'd asked her if anybody on the psychiatric staff might be willing to volunteer an opinion on the Davidson case for my book. She then mentioned a relative of hers who claimed the psychic ability to find missing things. His was the kind of psychic talent you read about being used by police to look for missing-presumed-dead bodies (although, thankfully, this guy hadn't been involved in anything quite so grim). Through the relative, I was referred to Dr. McMahon.

McMahon's doctorate was in the study of paranormal phenomena (apparently, you can major in this somewhere), and she helped manage a privately-funded Manhattan library dedicated to the field. She also had done some investigating of her own into psychic events, lectured on the paranormal, and had collaborated on a book intended to direct people away from bogus psychics and toward those who supposedly had something legitimate to offer.

Again, my movie-reinforced prejudices had poorly prepared me. Don't think Whoopi Goldberg in *Ghost*, or the geeky, super-serious paranormal investigators of *Poltergeist*. Joanne McMahon was distractingly attractive, professional, dressed like a corporate executive, and possessed of an absolutely charming sense of humor about her field of study:

"You're giving a lecture on after-death experiences and you see this little old lady in the front row break into tears and you *know* she's going to come up to you afterwards with a sad story about the ghost of somebody coming to visit her. And you're wondering, what am I supposed to *say* to this lady? And it happens *all* the time!"

According to McMahon, she often antagonized dedicated paranormal believers because she always approached possible psychic events with what she considered an appropriate scientific attitude: skepticism. The best way to prove something paranormal was "real," she felt, was to try like hell to *dis*prove it. What you *couldn't* disprove *had* to be real. Consequently, and much to the dismay of believers, she'd found a lot of so-called paranormal phenomena wasn't so paranormal: faulty wiring, ground water, squirrels in the attic. But, even if most of what she'd looked at had been write-offs, what kept her a believer – or at least open to extraordinary possibilities – were the few things, however small in number, "…that you can't explain."

I outlined the Davidson case for her and brought up the séances and how all the mediums seemed to have "fished" for revelations rather than experienced some sort of psychic epiphany. I asked if there were such a thing as true mediums.

There were, she said, she'd seen some at work. She also pointed out that, to be fair, different mediums get their insights in different ways. For some, it comes in flashes, while others may get a sense; it varied from one to the next.

"So how can you tell when you're dealing with a valid medium?"

She smiled. "They don't fish."

But she also pointed out how even true mediums, particularly ones dealing with the same "sitter" over a period of time, begin to "read" the sitter; they begin picking up cues from their subjects rather than from the spirits of the dead (shades of my palm-reading paralegal!). Some of the mediums may not even be consciously aware they're doing it; it's just a normal part of human communication.

"When people deal with a medium," McMahon said, "they come out amazed and go, 'He/she knew something about me *nobody* could know!' That's not true. Somebody *does* know. *You!* And a lot of mediums are incredibly good at picking that kind of thing up."

Much of what Joe Davidson had logged in his diary McMahon chalked up to "synchronicity." What about the flashing lights?

"Well, we *all* have that."

So, then, what *was* going on with the Davidsons?

"This sounds like grief," she said. "They have to let go."

There was still a lot of hemming and hawing going on over the contract after Christmas; too much, I thought. I expressed my frustration to my agent, and she expressed hers to the Davidsons. We were asked to be patient.

The longer this went on, the more resigned my agent and I were to the possibility-fast-becoming-probability the project wasn't going to happen. When word finally came from the Davidsons they were pulling the plug on the project, we weren't surprised.

Neither was Joanne McMahon.

I'd told her I'd be back in touch as, and if, the project developed so I could get ongoing feedback from her on whatever else I came across. When the Davidsons sent word the deal was dead, I gave the doctor a call to let her know.

She said considering the kind of book I'd been proposing – one challenging and testing the Davidsons' experiences – "I would've been surprised if they *had* gone ahead with it."

Samuel was alive for them, she said. Why would they want to challenge that?

The Good Book (Webster; not The Bible) says:

> *Faith: 1 a: allegiance to duty or a person:*
> *LOYALTY b (1): fidelity to one's promises (2)*
> *sincerity of intentions 2 a (1) belief and trust*
> *in and loyalty to God (2) belief in the*
> *traditional doctrines of a religion b (1) firm*
> *belief in something for which there is no proof*
> *(2) complete trust 3: something that is*
> *believed esp. with strong conviction esp: a*
> *system of religious beliefs.*

Let me tell you a little parable about faith.

It used to be an accepted article of Western faith that the sun and planets and the rest of the universe revolved around the earth. Along with the little we could divine from looking up at the stars moving through the night sky, this was a concept which made a certain amount of theological sense. We are – the thinking of the time went – the grandest of God's creations; everything *should* revolve around us! Then, along came Galileo and his made-it-myself telescope, and he reported, Sorry, folks (not a direct quote), it's the other way around; the Earth moves around the sun. In fact, we don't seem to be the center of *anything!*

To the Christian church of the time, this was not a scientific observation to be challenged, debated, tested, and then, based on the results of that process, accepted or discounted. To the Church faithful, removing God's pets from the center of Creation was nothing less than heresy. To defend this precept of the faith, the Church felt justified in telling Galileo if he didn't change his mind about what he saw through the telescope, he'd soon be solving the riddles of the universe face-to-face with The Creator. Galileo, whose allegiance to The Truth was not quite as strong as his allegiance to breathing, understandably recanted.

Just because Galileo didn't have the faith of your average Christian martyr didn't make him wrong, and just because the Church's faith was stronger than Galileo's didn't send the universe spinning around the Earth. The moral of the story is that Faith – despite the religious and spiritual connotations hanging around it – is not, as Webster points out, necessarily religious, spiritual, or even good.

Faith can cut two ways. The same book of faith that sustained Mother Teresa in her work with India's sick and poor also sustained Jim Jones, David Koresh, and similar Jeremiahs who also used scripture as the justification for their respective mini-apocalypses. Everybody from the late Jerry Falwell on the right to Bishop Spong on the left has bemoaned a world where we live, as Spong wrote in *Liberating the Gospels,* in "…an age of secularism, when the fires of faith and belief burn weakly…" I've argued that point with a long line of born-again Christian friends who also take the view that people have traded faith for reason, science, logic, self-indulgence, hedonism, psychology, etc., and that's why we have wars and adultery and poverty and drug abuse and the whole litany of contemporary social ills.

But my feeling – especially since 9/11 – is maybe there's too *much* faith in the world. Find a great evil in human history – and most of the small ones as well – and behind it you'll like as not find people motivated by great faith who believe they are carrying out God's will (or manifest destiny or some other crusade-justifying bit of belief). After all, it wasn't secular humanism, or the scientific method, or the product of reasoned argument that flew planes into the Twin Towers, or blew up a downtown office building in Oklahoma City even though there was a children's day care center inside, or judged AIDS to be God's punishment on homosexuals, or motivated people to ethnically cleanse men, women and children in Serbia, Darfur, Holocaust Europe, Uganda, or America's Old West. That – and too much more – was all the product of firmly embraced, deeply rooted, fervent, unshakeable faith…and maybe we could use a little less of it.

Editorialist William Raspberry, touching on the spiritual hunger most of us have to believe in *something*, wrote "…96 percent of us profess a belief in some universal spirit that transcends our physicality…" And that hunger, according to bestselling author and spiritualist teacher Marianne Williamson, may be greater now than it's ever been. "People are looking for hope today," she said in a 2016 article on miracles in *Parade*, "because the world is so filled with fear and chaos."

So, unsurprisingly, the various forms that belief takes, though motivated by spiritual hunger, seems ultimately governed by another human hunger: comfort.

Any idiot can tell you the only healthy way to lose weight is to exercise and eat healthy. But, every time there's some easier cure-all – fen-phen, the Scarsdale Diet, Jenny Craig, lo-fat/sugarless/all-natural foods, liposuction – it's, "Screw the diet, get rid of my treadmill; just gimme some of *that!*"

You can tell people that urban problems are the result of the loss of good-paying industrial jobs in geographically convenient zones, an inevitable result of globalization as blue-collar industries migrate to countries with cheap labor which, in turn, produces an erosion of the urban tax base resulting in a deteriorating infrastructure, particularly in the area of education which, in turn, perpetuates an urban population of undereducated, low-skilled labor in a job market becoming increasingly high-tech and suburban, the end result being the employable leave the city, the underskilled are left behind, and the city continues to rot.

Yeah, you can tell people all that, but there's an awful lot of people who, when they hear it, are just going to shake their heads and tell you the *real* reason the cities falter is because too many niggers and spics live there. God knows, that's an easier idea to get your head around.

U.S. News & World Report columnist John Leo once wrote about this tendency of people, organizations, and even the press to deal with hot-button issues – from Tawana Brawley to the federal deficit – with these end-runs for the Comfort & Simplicity Zone. Leo described the attitude as, "Don't bother us with facts; we are busy having some important emotions." Invariably, whenever you get to what people believe – politically, socially, spiritually – you find they're *not* on a hunt for undeniable Truth...not if the truth makes them unhappy.

If you're gay and you're told homosexuality is a sin, you naturally enough don't want to believe you're on the invitee list for Hell so you find people who tell you it's ok to be gay. If you're told abortion is bad and you find yourself in a circumstance where you feel you need one, you find people who are "pro-choice." If you don't want to believe life on this planet is an incredible accident, which means our lives have no real purpose, no meaning, and we may very well be alone in the universe, you find people who tell you there's a Divine Plan at work and God loves you and every one of God's creations – including you – is special (or you start believing we're being visited by aliens).

We believe we're right when we make these choices, and we join churches and chat rooms and other similarly affirming groups who share what we believe to be right because nothing gives us confirmation in our rightness like hearing a bunch of other people espousing the same thing.

The alternative is to believe we're wrong, which means a lifetime of self-recrimination and unhappiness. By and large, people just don't find that an appetizing form of existence.

In Anne Puryear's *Stephen Lives!*, in nearly every account from the Guggenheims' *Hello From Heaven!*, and in the story of the Davidsons, I kept coming across – like the hook from a Top Ten song everybody's humming – the word "comfort." Comfort, it appeared, was the emotional spine of the paranormalists. Subjects and psychics alike shared respective "messages of comfort": life doesn't end when you die, your loved ones are ok and hunky dory in the afterlife. Somebody much loved may have died before their time, but there was still a happy ending to their story.

If comfort is the paranormal's main commodity, then absolution was the other half of its regular "two-fer" offer. When loved ones came for a visit from The Other Side, they always seemed to bring an assuaging message with them. It wasn't just that *they* were ok, but *you* were ok, too. You were a good mother/father/friend/son/daughter/sister/brother/husband/wife, and if things hadn't always been the best between you, it wasn't anybody's fault. You'd tried your best, all was forgiven and/or forgotten, and so on and so forth.

What you *never* read or heard of was a soul coming back to tell somebody that, "Hey, in case I didn't get a chance to say it when I was alive, you were a rat bastard. In fact, you're *still* a rat bastard! You're the kind of rat bastard Hell was built for, and I *know* because I've seen it!" You never heard in these tales of visitation of someone returning to declare an old acquaintance to be a cheating spouse, an untrustworthy friend, an uncaring parent, or a deceitful sibling, and that it would take the remainder of the offender's lifetime on his/her knees begging forgiveness to square accounts.

Long after my relationship with the Davidsons had faded, all of this echoed back to me when I caught a pay-per-view special starring a psychic. I guessed she must've been a psychic of some standing since you don't get your own pay-per-view special unless your name has enough commercial draw to make it worthwhile. As for her bonafides, I'd heard she had, supposedly, helped out the police on investigations.

On this special she wasn't helping cops find fiends and killers and missing persons. Instead, she was helping a parade of wounded souls – jilted lovers, bereaved loved ones, frustrated aspirants – with advice and counsel about their troubled lives, kind of a psychic Oprah Winfrey.

If I had to extract a theme from this paranormal "concert," it was there's few personal problems you can't attribute to wounds suffered in previous existences. A woman kept picking lousy men not because she had self-esteem issues or co-dependence problems, but because she'd always been getting crapped on as a French girl in the 16th Century. These reincarnation diagnostics were invariably followed by firm and loving advice along the lines of "let it go" and "get past it," iced with an aphorism about what a nice person the subject was and how you should be good to yourself.

Even if you buy into this reincarnated dysfunction business, I don't see how knowing this necessarily makes your present existence any better. Even everyday non-supernatural therapy doesn't end with the epiphany that mommy didn't love you; finding out what went wrong is just the beginning of the repair process. But, for subjects featured in this show, this sudden understanding bestowed by Her Wisdomness was, evidently, a salving experience, and the subjects acted like the psychic's thirty-second diagnosis did more healing than a series of weekly sessions with a therapist.

I will always remember one young woman – sweet, almost shy — who sat with the psychic, troubled by her inability to actively pursue her dream of being a dancer. She just couldn't get herself in gear. The psychic, as per usual, told the sitter the problem wasn't with her, but the damage done to her in a previous life, and now that she'd been made aware of this she could go on out there and do what she wanted to do and everything was going to be fine.

While I may have been needlessly caustic in my thinking, I couldn't help but look at that girl's fragile little ankles and then at her expansive hips and think, "Sister, you'd be doing this kid a big favor if you also mentioned it wouldn't hurt to drop fifty pounds."

"Logically, there is no way to improve the odds on a random drawing with 9,366,819 to one odds," Roger Pinkham, a professor of statistics and probability theory at Stevens Institute of Technology said in a newspaper story about lottery players' obsession with systems of choosing lottery numbers. "But human beings are wonderfully clever at creating explanations for things, even when there isn't an explanation…People have a need to find order in chaos."

Read The Bible, The Koran, the Tao, the Bhagavad Gita, anything you can grab on Hinduism, Sufism, Unitarian Universalism, karma, reincarnation, mysticism, astrology, Native American shamanism, and any other spiritual ism you can find. Add in the gamut of political philosophical isms and ologies, throw in the whole buffet of paranormal phenomena. Human history is full of the search for something – *anything* – to tell us there's a plan at work, something accounting for such unaccountables as the Holocaust, 9/11, thalidomide babies, and bad dreams; something to tell us we're in better hands than our own, that everything will come out right in the end. Like on TV.

Faith is what we use to chink the holes in theologies and creeds, the paradoxes in scriptures, the dissonance between our heart-held beliefs and what our eyes see around us. Faith co-opts problems, situations, and circumstances into The Plan, making them signs, omens, premonitions. Faith is a belief system's way of telling disciples, "You've got to trust me on this"; it's what we use to put reason on hold when reason – by dint of our fears, insecurities, or perhaps most pointedly, our hungers – isn't enough.

As the century changed, that need, those hungers seemed stronger than ever.

Maybe for no reason other than we have ten fingers and ten toes, we imbue round numbers with a certain gravitas. Any hack salesman can tell you price tags read $1.99 because the one-cent bump to $2.00 – in our heads – becomes much larger than a penny. We segment our history into theme decades, like the '50s, the '60s, and so on, even though the cultural events we use to identify those eras don't really fit into those neat ten-year spans. But, the methodology does organize the fits-and-starts of history into a nice, orderly flow. And, as we came up on the year 2000, well, that's wasn't just a decade closing, but the end of a *century!* That's a *really* round number; a really *heavy* number! It *must* be significant! It *must* have *meaning!* Maybe it signals some great *ending!* Maybe some great *beginning!* Maybe *both!*

We felt it had to mean something because we needed it to. Because if it did, in *that* meaning, maybe we could find *our* meaning.

The arbitrariness of all this imbued meaning became ever clearer in the closing days of 1999 as one magazine and newspaper story after another pointed out it was only the end of the century on the Gregorian calendar; the Moslem calendar hadn't yet reached the year 2000, and the calendars of eastern civilizations had long since passed it. In fact, even on the Gregorian calendar, 1999 was not the true last year of the century. The century wouldn't officially end until the close of the *following* year when the clock turned to 2001.

But more people read their daily astrology than the science page, so, as the 20th Century's clock ran out, there was a run on the spirituality department before the perceived closing time. Promise Keepers, Heavens Gaters, Million Man (and Woman) Marches, family values, goddess worship, survivalists, Satanists, Wiccans, UFOlogists, white separatists, psychic daters...by the time the big ball came down in Times Square, there was a palpable feeling you'd better be holding on to *something* because, with all those zeroes, the end of the century couldn't possibly be just another day.

Which, as we all know, is exactly what it turned out to be.

In a newspaper story on the human fixation with the number three, Cornell University psychology professor Thomas Gilovich said people tend to believe what they want to believe and will see order even in random sequences. I thought of the Davidsons when I read that, of how the lights in their home flicker and they see in it a sign from Samuel.

I, on the other hand, believe it's a short in the wiring of an old building.

But...

Even if it *is* just a short in the wiring, who's to say Samuel's spirit isn't taking advantage of some bad wiring to send a message?

People believe what they want to believe, and belief, as John Taylor wrote, "is itself irrational."

I had proposed to the Davidsons a book which would look critically at their story leaving the question of "Is it or isn't it real?" for the reader to answer. I was righter than I knew in my approach, but for all the wrong reasons.

For me, the tactic had been something of a cop-out, a way of avoiding a conflict between what I was pretty sure I'd wind up believing about the case (short in the wiring), and what the Davidsons obviously and fervently believed (message from Samuel). But, in looking back, I now see there would've been no more honest way to approach the subject. When you get into belief, what's "real" and "true" is as real and true as you believe it to be. And, if you have damned little that's tangible to prove your case, well, your critics often have just as damned little to disprove it.

That's it. No great final insight, no mystical Gestalt. Not even a satisfying ending to the story. This is real life, and real life rarely provides a neat dramatic arc and thrilling climax. I will resist the human tendency pointed out by Pinkham and Gilovich to impose an artificial construct here.

The Davidsons still come to mind from time to time. I see something – like that psychic's pay-per-view display – read something, maybe the name of one of the mediums the Davidsons dealt with comes up, and I think of them.

On the eve of the millennium, Joe Davidson got an article published about his and his wife's communications with Samuel. The article ran in a magazine dedicated to that kind of material, all of its stories written by fellow believers, to be read by people who were fellow believers. Joe sent my agent and me a copy of the article. I guess he must've sensed my skepticism even in that first and only meeting because I detected, in his little cover note, a touch of I-told-you-so, as if the fact his story was now in print was some kind of validation of his and his wife's experiences.

Like I said: people believe what they want to believe. Or, in some cases, what they *need* to believe.

When I think back to Joe and Mary, I wonder how the experience would've played out – professionally and personally — if I had managed to dope out the full proposal then draft a manuscript. Still, I was grateful for the experience because it pushed me to ask some questions of myself, look at why I think what I think and how I think it. Everybody should go through that exercise once in a while; a psychological/spiritual tune-up.

I didn't then, nor do I now, believe in what the Davidsons told me they were living with, but I have shelved (most of) my pooh-pooh attitude. There's a lot to be skeptical of in the Davidson' experience, but nothing to mock. The love of their son – before and after his death – and their obvious grief over his loss is too real to allow any kind of condescension.

There's even a part of me envying their situation.

At a time when people are starving for something to believe in, something to guide them through the chaos that day-to-day living has devolved into, the Davidsons have found it. They have an unwavering, unswerving faith in that belief, and however wrongheaded anyone may think they are, they're doing no one any harm.

I don't know; maybe that kind of delusion – if it is a delusion – does do some kind of psycho-emotional damage over the long haul to the people who hold it, but at the Davidsons' advanced age, I'm inclined to doubt the downsides will kick in before they've joined Samuel. In the meantime, delusion or not, they have found not just solace, but a sense of wholeness, an ability to enjoy life, and a fearlessness toward death. All of us have a primal fear of the dark, and Death threatens to be the greatest darkness of all. The Davidsons have found their nightlight.

Those of us who haven't found such a light – or who've lost it – continue to stumble through the gloom, looking for something to chase away the shadows, to make us feel warm and safe; something to give us the will to get up in the morning and face another day; something to keep the boogy man away at night.

"Faith and doubt both are needed – not as antagonists but working side by side – to take us around the unknown curve."

Lillian Smith

ACKNOWLEDGMENTS

"Furlough, November 1944" first appeared in the November 2017 issue of *Ovunque Siamo*.

"Brad's Office" first appeared in the 2016 issue of *Alligator Juniper*.

"The General" first appeared in *KYSO Flash*, issue #5, spring 2016.

"Tides" first appeared in *KYSO Flash*, winter 2015 issue.

"A Small Piece of History" first appeared in *PenSpark*, 2010.

"Post Mortem" first appeared in *PenSpark*, 2010.

Bill Mesce, Jr. is an award-winning author and playwright as well as a screenwriter. He is an adjunct instructor at several colleges in his native New Jersey.